The Knot

Eva Figes was born in Berlin and came to England
just before the outbreak of the Second World War.
She won the Guardian Fiction prize with
Winter Journey. Her other novels include
*Light, Waking, The Seven Ages, Ghosts,
The Tree of Knowledge* and *The Tenancy*.
She lives in London.

The Knot

Eva Figes

Minerva

A Minerva Paperback
THE KNOT

First published in Great Britain 1996
by Sinclair-Stevenson
This Minerva edition published 1997
by Mandarin Paperbacks
an imprint of Reed International Books Ltd
Michelin House, 81 Fulham Road, London SW3 6RB
and Auckland, Melbourne, Singapore and Toronto

Copyright © 1996 by Eva Figes
The author has asserted her moral rights

A CIP catalogue record for this title
is available from the British Library
ISBN 0 7493 9542 7

www.minervabooks.com

Typeset in Imprint
Printed and bound in Great Britain
by Cox & Wyman Ltd, Reading, Berkshire

Contents

~ Part One ~

I

Not merely sound, but now light, coming and going. Blurs, shadows, a sudden dazzling without sound, no thudding, no voice, appearing silently from nowhere, or vanishing. No pattern to the appearing and disappearing, no beat, no smell. A shadow which moves, wavering, another which does not stir. The waving shadow breathes a sigh, the inert shadow makes no sound.

Bbbb.

The unmoving shadow says nothing. Just continues to stand. Huge, with straight edges. It will not speak to me, not moving. I kick, wave my arms. A tiny silver sound near my ear. Kick, wave, so the sound returns.

Dddd.

Speaking, words forming a voice. I know this shadow, it moves towards me, speaking, bending forward, mouth opening and shutting, being held, being lifted, everything shifting, shapes, shadows, wavering between bright and dark.

Mumum.

The smell, the thud thud under roundness, the mouth speaking. Looking up, into the two eyes

3

looking down. Sound forming, reaching me, a round mumum smelling of succour, for me, for me. Soothing sound flowing deep into me, lulling the craving, the loss. For now I hear it, thud thud, thud thud, and the harsh shadows, the harsh light converges to soothing, smoothing surges of grey.

2

She is coming. Footsteps, sudden bright light, now the sound of her voice. She bends down, her mouth opening, sounds coming out, for me. Her eyes looking down at me. I am in them, small, safe. The words shaping towards their end, soothing, lulling. I smell her too.

I smile back, screeching, kicking, arms waving. The tiny silver sound near my ear. When she brings her head forward I put my fingers in her mouth, between her lips, where the words come from, warm and wet. Now she is sucking, licking. I watch to see what happens, now her mouth is shut, holding my fingers. Suddenly she lets go.

Boo!

She laughs, I laugh too.

Up, I am up now, looking over her shoulder, passing the things that stand still, that have nothing to say. Down, going down. She is still talking to me, steadily, step by step, here we go, down, this is down, each word rounding familiarly as we go, now, now.

Pictures pass as we go, eyes looking at me, but the mouth says nothing, not now, not then. I watch them being left behind.

Out.

Out is a sudden burst of light, so bright I must turn, blinking.

Look.

I try to see, she points to where the light is moving, long sharp splinters coming through tiny shapes, dancing, moving about, speaking to each other. I do not know what they are saying.

Pretty.

This is pretty, all this stirring and whispering, this odour. I do not know what it is saying.

See?

It is jumping about. It is looking at me with two round eyes. Suddenly it goes up into the air, vanishing. I look at her.

Bird, she says bird.

I look into the empty space where it was.

Gone.

All things stirring in the bright light, shadows, things, smells too, coming and going. Something with no eyes, no mouth, drifts up into the air, silently. Suddenly, down on the ground, a black thing with gleaming eyes and several legs is coming our way. I watch it and, when it is near, point.

Shoo!

She is angry with it, I can tell. It runs away, fast.

3

Shoo jumps off the table and runs out. I want to see him, but he has gone. Out. Where everything is moving. I know everything is moving: I can see the shapes dancing about on the floor, making patterns of light and dark. I watch the shadows moving. I can feel them blowing on my face. I cannot follow him. I hear the singing, far off, high, shrill as splintering light, blowing through the open door. I want to be like Shoo, running about, lightly, nearly flying. In and out, jumping up and down, nobody hears him. Shoo is lucky. He knows it, and looks at me strangely, with mean yellow eyes. If Mumum had seen him up on the table she would have been cross, trying to hit him, but missing. Yelling at him. Shoo is quick.

But Mumum is out of sight. She is not far off, I can hear her singing, picking things up, putting things down. I hear a bell ring. Ringring. Mumum is speaking to somebody, but I do not know who. I can only hear her, nobody else. She has forgotten Baba. Everybody has gone off, leaving me by myself. I hear her laughing. Nobody is talking to me. I am stuck.

I yell, but nobody hears me. I hold a thing, which bangs loudly. Nobody comes. I throw the thing on the floor. It moves a bit, then stops. Now I have nothing to throw. I look at it, but it will not come back. It just lies there. I yell loudly now, without stopping.

Mumum comes through the door. I have been yelling loudly enough, long enough.

What is it?

I peer down at the floor.

She picks up the thing from the floor and puts it in my hand. I throw it down, watch it land on the floor. It is not moving now. I want to keep trying it, see how it drops, but Mumum has her back to me, doing something, not looking.

Aa. Aa.

What is it?

She puts something round my neck. I resist, cross now, trying to look at the thing on the floor.

Soon.

She puts down a spoon. I bang it, put it in my mouth, throw it on the floor. I cannot see where it fell.

Anna!

I think Anna means no, if spoken loudly and sharply. Its meaning is forever changing, it hangs vague as a cloud, coming and going. Spoken softly it means other things, for the hurt to go away. I never know when I will hear it, or how it will sound when I do. But hear it I will. Anna is not stuck to any one thing, not spoon or food or toy. It comes out of nowhere, suddenly, uttered without warning, expressively, like a shout, or a clapping of hands. It might be joyous or stern, spoken loudly out of nowhere, or soothingly close to my ear, but each time with a space around it, mysterious, which I cannot fathom. I look at the mouth which is speaking, following the eyes, but they are not looking at anything in particular, just back at me. Nor are the hands pointing, holding up something, or if, then it might be anything, spoon or food or toy.

No. Anna is no such thing. Anna is a mood, the light which is constantly changing, now dark, or grey, or a bright golden dazzle hitting things suddenly, running across the floor. Just now it is heavy cloud, dull and brooding. She is frowning, no light in her eyes, refusing to look at me. She is getting down under the table to retrieve the spoon. I watch her, not giving it to me, throwing it into the sink with a loud clatter. I have nothing to hold, or suck, or throw. But I do not cry out. I am wary of the dark cloud, the clattering spoon, the expression on her face. I watch, wait.

4

Gone.

Nothing else. He was here, and now he is not. I look round the room and it is empty. I listen, but hear nothing. Only the white thing humming. Sometimes I hear him coming. Now everything is still. The white thing has stopped too. She is holding the spoon up, not moving. Sometimes I hear him calling out, but not now. I turn my head to where he was standing, but he has gone. This is mysterious. I look at her, but she says nothing, just holds the spoon to

8

my mouth. Why? She is not telling me, just saying open up, bringing the spoon to my mouth. I do not know why he is not here, suddenly. I am not hungry, do not want the food. I want to see him, see where he is. Why is he not in the room? I keep my mouth shut tight then, when she keeps pushing, shake my head, spit.

Anna.

I hear the dark cloud rumbling from afar. He is not here. She is, holding the spoon. I open my mouth, swallow. And again.

Good girl, she says, soothingly. The white thing purrs. Sunlight is in the room, in her voice. She is scraping the dish.

All gone.

Triumph in the words, sung out. Her triumph, our triumph, my reward coming.

Up. We are moving. She is holding me. I see the world from a long way up, looking down. Everything is moving, freely. The floor is far off, tilting, everything sways.

Out. She is taking me out. I might see Shoo.

For a moment I see nothing. The light is everywhere, too bright. Everything is moving, stirring, the light is touching my face. I look round and see everything blowing, swaying about, small things fly up, then fall down. Her hair is flying, getting into her mouth, tickling my skin. She laughs. The light is dancing about.

Look at the tree, she says, holding me under the big thing which whispers and sighs and moves to and fro. In it the light is playing hide and seek, darting through, now here, now there. Too bright. So bright it splinters into colours. Sound comes from the tree. Is it laughter? Lots of little things moving to and fro. Mumum picks one for me and I put it in my mouth, trying it. She pulls it out. Holds it in her hand. I take it from her, look at it. Suddenly it goes up into the air.

Gone, she says, laughing.

Tree. Mumum puts Baba down under it. Now she is gone. I look up into the big tree. It is whispering, moving to and fro. What is it doing, saying? I see no mouth, just lots of eyes shining, lots of fingers moving, stirring, throwing the light about. I hear no words, just whispers sighing, far off. Hush, it is saying hush. Or is it? Look, it says, look. See how I toss the light to and fro, juggling. Peepo. The light playing peepo between its fingers. It is blowing on me, so it is not too hot. Tossing me up and down in the light going to and fro, the arms swaying: hush, baby, hush. Singing, singing. I hear the words now, how they run into each other, light into dark, into sleeping.

5

No.

I hear her voice coming from behind me. She is in the room. She is always in the room when I am doing this, the word following me about. I have just managed to pull myself up. Now the word is getting longer. It gets longer as I get further away, and the sound begins to alter. But I go on. Now I have begun moving, I go on. Touching, feeling, finding out.

It is near my hand now, exuding light and colour. Standing still. I feel it is hard and cold. Now it is wobbling.

Suddenly I feel myself flying backwards. She is lifting me up. The thing is far off. Her foot is nearby, with something hard and shiny on it. I pull but it does not come off. It resists, making no sound. Nearby is stuff which I know will not resist. I pull, it falls to the ground, crinkling, dividing easily, bits falling, not hard, not sharp, not making a loud or alarming noise. It tastes bad, so I spit it out, but it keeps doing different things, changing shape, bending, endlessly complying.

But now she is suddenly picking me up. I am on her lap. No, she is saying. This time the word is near, not far off, blowing softly on my head. Cooing, pulling me in to her body. I hear it constantly, and it is forever pulling me back, to her, as if it were string. She is jiggling me up and down on her lap, holding me. I try to pull the thing on her arm, but it will not come off. I keep tugging.

As she bounces me up and down, she begins to say words, which bounce in rhythm. The word gets louder, the bounces go higher. This is fun. Words bouncing me up and down, not pulling me back on a string. I laugh, so she starts doing it again. And again.

Enough, she says, putting me down. Picking up the crinkly stuff, putting it back from where I pulled it out. I watch her doing it, begin to pull.

No, she says, putting her hand in the way. I desist. Look up at her. She is shaking her head. I shake my head too. I know this game. She is smiling. We are both smiling, shaking our heads.

6

Mummy has left me in the garden. Thomas is in the garden too. I watch him walking, with his tail up. I sit under the tree, eating my biscuit. The tree is very big, bigger than Mummy or Daddy. I am not big. I am Baby, and I am eating a biscuit. Teddy is in the garden too, lying down. He never eats, but Thomas eats things. Now he is coming towards me, on his legs. I offer him my biscuit, but he does not have any hands, only feet. So Thomas drinks with his tongue, not with a cup. Mummy puts a saucer on the floor, with milk in it, and he goes lap-lap. I hold my cup with both hands.

Thomas sniffs my biscuit, then walks off. His tail goes from side to side. I do not have a tail. He looks up into the tree, which is so big. I hear birds up in the tree, talking to each other. I do not know what they are saying. Thomas runs up into the tree and the birds fly off. Thomas can do this, having so many legs, but he cannot fly. I cannot fly either, nor Mummy, though she can reach up into the tree. Once she picked a leaf, and gave it to Baby. Now I am sitting under the tree, in the garden, and she is in the house. Nobody is with me, not even Thomas, who has run away. I can hear the birds talking. Teddy is with me, but he never talks. Teddy is just lying, looking up into the tree.

The grass is green, so are the leaves up on the tree. My ball is yellow, so is Teddy, but the ball has red bits on it, which go round. Baby is wearing a blue dress. The sky is blue too. I can see blue flowers. Thomas is brown, but he has white bits, his tummy mostly. The sky has white bits, but they come and go, running away, flying, but not as fast as the birds. Birds fly so fast, I can hardly see them go. Up into the sky, then back. The tree touches the sky too. So can my Daddy, but he has to reach up. But the tree is so big, it does not need to reach up. It is reaching up without trying.

The birds stay up in the tree now. They are not flying. I can hear them arguing. The tree is waving about, trying to shake them off. Shoo, it is saying, but the birds stay up in it, just laughing. Singing loudly. A fly is sitting on my biscuit. Shoo, I say, waving it about, and it has gone. Baby is big, the fly is teenyweeny, so it flew off. It will do what I say. Thomas is big, he will not do what I tell him. If I say shoo he just walks about. When Mummy says shoo he runs off. Thomas does not even have to say shoo when he runs after birds. They fly off in a hurry.

I am all alone in the garden. Everything is still, only a bee is humming nearby. Everything is very big, Baby is small. I pull up a flower. It is yellow. I pull it to bits. Now my hands are yellow. Shoo, I say to the bee, waving at it, but it is still flying about, even though I am big and it is not.

I can hear a daddy singing, but I cannot see him. It is not my daddy. I can hear the bee, but I cannot see it now. Everything is suddenly very slow. Nobody is doing anything except for the bee, which is crawling in the grass now. I pull up a white flower, with a yellow bit in the middle. It is not saying anything, and I pull it to bits.

The white flower has a name, but I do not know what it is. Everything is called something. Everybody is. Baby is Anna. We call our pussy Thomas. My mummy has a name: it is Susan. I think Daddy has a name, but I do not know what it is. Ellen is called Ellen. She helps Mummy in the house. If I ask her, she helps me with my house. It is not a real house, but a pretend house. It is really a box, but not when I am in it. My dolly has a name: it is Helen. I decide when Helen is hungry, and when she has to go to bed. Helen cannot really talk, so I talk for her.

7

Lavender blue, dilly dilly, lavender green, when I am king dilly dilly, you shall be queen. Seen. Green. I shall be queen. I shall be green. That is a good joke. Nobody is green. The tree is green. You shall be a green queen, tree. I am talking to the trees. The leaves in the trees seem to whisper Louise. Louise has a yellow frock. Frock, sock. Yellow socks. Buttercups are yellow, so is butter. Butternutter. I like butter. My chin goes yellow. So do my fingers. Butterfingers. Butterfingers! That's what she calls me sometimes. My fingers go yellow. Yellowbellow. Daisies are yellow in the middle. Lazy daisy, lazy daisy. They shut up for the night. In the morning, when I am up, they are still shut. Shut up! Shut up, lazy daisy. Rosy posy. Nosy rosy posy. Ring-a-ring-a-rosy. Sing-a-sing-a-rosy posy. Roses are red, or pink, or white. I can make pink by mixing up red and white. I could paint the roses a different colour. Painting the world with sunshine! The sun shines east, the sun shines west, I know where the sun shines best. West rhymes with best. Sun rhymes with . . . fun. Sun and fun, sun and fun. Everything rhymes with something. House with mouse. Housemouse. Hickory dickory dock, the mouse runs up the clock. Dock with clock. Sock!

The clock goes bong. Ding dong bell, pussy in the well. Well with bell. What is a well, exactly? Pussy fell in it. Fell in the well. I have some wellingtons, but you could not fall into those, no. Much too small. Fall, small! I am small, I will fall. You are tall, and you will fall too.

Ding dong bell. Bell, belly. Belly button. I will put a buttercup in my belly button. It falls out. It is yellow now, so my belly likes butter. Helen likes butter too, but only pretend. She is lying down. Her eyes are shut, so Helen is sleeping. I am lying down, but I am not sleeping. I am looking up into the sky. High into the sky. Why is it so high? The clouds fly by. It makes me feel dizzy. A ladybird is crawling up my arm. It is not a lady, or a bird, but it is a ladybird. It can fly, too. Ladybird, ladybird fly away home, your house is on fire your children are gone. It did not hear me. It does not understand what I say. Now it is crawling on my finger. My finger is very big and the ladybird is very small. My finger is not really big, but the ladybird thinks so. She does not even know it is my finger. She thinks it is something else. I will put her in my box. Go on, ladybird, go inside. I am not going to hurt you, so don't be frightened. I'll look after you. It flies off. It did not understand what I said. It is too small to talk. I can talk now, so I am not a baby. Little ladybabybird. I was not going to hurt you. I try speaking to tiny things in a tiny voice, so they will understand better, and not be scared off. The words sound high and squeaky, but it flew off anyhow. Suddenly. It keeps its wings hidden, so you cannot tell what it is going to do.

I will put a daisy in my box. It cannot fly off. We also have big daisies in our garden, but I am not allowed to pick those. Why? I asked. Because, she said. Because of the wonderful things he does. We're off to see the wizard. I will pretend this is the yellow brick road. The wonderful wizard of Oz. I must not tread here. Why? I asked. Because, she said. Because because because. I don't think she saw me. Anyhow, I didn't mean to. Because of the wonderful things he does. I wish my name was Dorothy. I will pretend it is. I am following the yellow brick road. Thomas, you can be Toto. Don't run off, I have to pick you up. Thomas! I mean, Toto! Come back. He hardly ever does what I say. But dogs do what you tell them. Toto would, mostly. I wish we had a dog, not Thomas. Helen, you had better be Toto. Or would you rather be the scarecrow? You want to be Toto? I thought so. Don't be scared, it's only a hurricane.

It is hot. The sun is shining and it is hot. It is summer now, so we are having a picnic, not lunch. She puts cups and plates under the tree. I don't want to sit there, I say. You must, she says. Sit in the shade. Why? I ask. Because, she says. Because too much sun is bad for you. You will get a headache. I haven't got a headache. But you will. I won't. Sit down and don't argue. I'm not arguing, only saying. Sit down and eat your lunch. Not lunch, picnic, you said we were having a picnic. The picnic is just bits of food cut up, tomatoes and cucumber and cheese, and now I am not hungry. I'm not hungry, I say. Yes you are. I don't want lunch, I want a picnic. Now you're being silly. I'm not silly, you are. I pretend to cry. I lean up against the tree, watching her out of the corner of my eye. But she is laughing. I am thirsty, and there is apple juice. My tummy is rumbling and the cheese is cut up into little squares, which is fun, and tasty. She is laughing, so it is easy to stop pretending and sit down. Now it is a picnic. We are sitting on a blanket, and she is smiling, and we are using our fingers to eat. She has no shoes on, nor have I. I can see tiny hairs on her legs. My juice is lovely and cold. She has freckles on her arms, and hair under them. Juice from the tomatoes runs down my chin, and on to my shirt. What a mess. I can see the tiny seeds which will grow into baby tomatoes. Will they grow in my tummy? No, they have to grow in the earth, nothing is going to

17

grow in your tummy. But the baby grows in yours. Yes. Can I listen to it? Not now, when you've finished eating.

I go on munching, swallowing, looking out to the bright sun burning all round. Sitting under the tree, the shade is touching us. It is running over her face as though it was water. Now she is lying down, and I lie down too. The sky, the trees are humming with things I do not know. Grass is tickling me too, running through my hair. The bees in the trees. Louise. The leaves in the trees. Sun running through them. Through my hair, all sorts of colours, looking through my eyelashes, misty, bits of rainbow. I can hear the baby growing. Thud thud.

8

It is autumn now, not summer. I can tell it is autumn: I have to wear warm clothes and socks, and the garden looks sad. Ellen takes me to nursery school in the mornings. We play in groups: I play with Sally and Martha and Simon. Sometimes we sing songs, but I have to sing the words all the other children sing, or my teacher, whose name is Barbara, says 'Anna' very loudly, and if I go on doing it she makes me stand out in front. Sometimes I forget, and do it anyhow, even though Barbara gets cross. She says it puts the others off, and that I do it to make them laugh. It is true that Sally, and sometimes Simon too, start laughing, but this is not why I do it, though I could. I do not really know why I do it. When I am by myself I do it all the time, adding bits, changing things round for fun, just so long as it fits. But Barbara says no: this will not do. There are right words and wrong words, and we all have to sing the right ones. Together. How would it sound, she asks, if everybody in the group was singing different words? Funny, says Simon, and both he and Sally start laughing. Martha is not laughing. Martha never says anything out loud. She is shy. Sometimes I give Martha things, and she says thank you, in a whisper. Simon hardly ever says thank you. He thinks it is sissy. But it is rude not to. When he came to my party and got his present he would not say thank you and his mother said if he did not, he would have to give it back. Simon just stood there, pulling a face and not looking up. 'What do you say?' she kept saying. Everybody knows what you have to say, and every-body was watching. Simon was being difficult. It is difficult when you start doing something and do not know how to stop, even though you want to. In the end he began to cry, and everybody felt sorry for him, even the grownups, so he got his present without saying anything. He says he did it, only very quickly, so nobody heard. Usually Simon thinks crying is sissy.

It is autumn now. Ellen says you know it is autumn when the leaves fall off the trees. Why do they fall off? Ellen does not know, she says they just do. Walking through them is fun. I love the sound they make: swish swosh. Swish swosh. I collect the nicest ones. I brought a leaf to Barbara, and she held it up for everybody to see. I chose it because it was bright red and yellow. Leaves that fall off are not green any more, like they were in the summer. I do not know why. Barbara says that trees which drop their leaves in the autumn are called de-ci-du-us. Why? I ask. Simon wants to know why too. Because, she says. Then says: because they drop their leaves in the autumn. She says she thinks my leaf is very pretty. She says trees which keep their leaves on all the time are called evergreen. I do not ask why. Not because she might get cross if I interrupt too much. This word is easy. It means they are green all the time. All the year round, she says. I went up to the front to ask for my leaf back. Afterwards I let Martha hold it.

It is still autumn. After autumn it will be winter, says Ellen, not summer, not hot. She says it will not be summer for a long, long time. Yesterday was autumn. Today it is autumn. It will be autumn tomorrow too. And even the day after that. It has been raining, and the street is wet. So is the garden. I cannot go out, even in my wellingtons. The leaves which fell down are all mushy, and dirty. Ellen told me there is an evergreen in our garden. Where? I say. There, she says, touching the window. It is very dark, hardly green at all. It is a bush, I say, not a tree. Well, she says, maybe. I want to know what it is called, but Ellen is not sure. Perhaps it's a rhododendron, she says. A rhododo, I say, laughing. Hello, rhodo-dodo, I shout, putting my mouth to the glass, but it just stands there, in the wet, looking glum.

Ellen is washing up. I do not know what to do.

How long till Mummy gets back? I ask. About an hour, says Ellen, looking at the clock. Will it be a long hour or a short hour? Ellen says nothing. An hour can be ever so quick, or just go on and on, and nobody says which it is going to be. They just say: an hour, which is like saying nothing at all. So if I am doing something really good I suddenly have to stop it. But if I am all ready for the next hour to come, it doesn't, even though I am waiting for it.

What is an hour? I ask Ellen, but she is not looking at me. She is drying her hands. An hour is when I go home, she tells me. Her head is in the cupboard. She is not talking properly now, just saying any old thing. Grownups say any old thing when they are busy doing other things. Ellen is putting up the ironing board. *Ellen*, I say very loudly, stamping my foot. Ellen puts down the iron and shows me the blue clock. When, she says, this hand has gone all the way round, then it will be an hour. I sit down at the table, watching the big hand. It is not moving. I tell Ellen. She says it is, only very slowly. I begin to cry. She calls me silly. I'm not silly, I shout. You're silly. The clock is silly.

I go into the front room, where Ellen is not. Nobody is in the front room, which is grey and empty. Nobody is walking past in the street, which is grey and wet. Nobody is coming, nothing is happening.

Everything in the world is very still. Nothing is moving, or making a sound. There is only me, and I am not moving, or making a sound. I am staring through the window, and nothing in the whole world is going on. Grey and wet, grey and wet. The evergreen goes drip drip. I am breathing. I can feel myself breathing as I lean against the back of the sofa. I might stop. Sometimes I try to stop breathing, but then I feel like bursting. Things are breathing, but very quietly. The clouds are breathing. Thomas is breathing on the chair. I can see his back going up and down. He is sleeping. He should not be sitting on the chair, but I will let him. Thomas is sleeping, the world is sleeping, breathing and sleeping. Nobody is doing things. I am watching, listening. I am looking, at the wet glass, through the window to the grey sky, to the street where nothing is moving. I just am.

9

It is dark. I do not know how long till I can get up. I can get up when the bell in my clock rings, but not till then. It is very quiet, so I think they are still asleep. I do not know how long I have to wait. This is boring, so I tell myself things. What did I do yesterday? I count up all the things, those I remember. Yesterday I did a painting of our house. Only then it was today. Now it is tomorrow, only it isn't. Now tomorrow is tomorrow. All the time. I never know what it is, but grownups say Tuesday or something, so they know. Only I don't know when Tuesday is.

Granny is coming soon. I do not know if it is this afternoon. She might come if it is Tuesday. There is no way of knowing whether it is Tuesday or not. I have a clock in my room, but it only tells when it is time to get up. She can remember before I was even born. She might have seen a dinosaur, just once, when they were roaming the earth. When they were roaming the earth, it says in my book. Granny says she went in a steam train, just like the one in my book. Now they are only in books, like dinosaurs. If I did not have any books, I would not know about them. Or I would have to go to a museum. Or Granny would have to tell me, but she only comes on Tuesdays, so I would not know very much.

I cannot see the hands on my clock and, anyhow, I cannot tell the time by looking at them. I have to wait for the bell to ring. I cannot hear them talking in the next room, or I could get up anyhow. I could pretend I had a bad dream, but I cannot remember any. I could make one up: I could say I thought I was being chased by a dinosaur, that it was trying to eat me up. That would be scary enough. But perhaps she would know I was making it up. Better not. It is bad to tell lies. It is bad to tell lies but it is all right to make up stories. I never know when they are making up stories, or if they are telling the truth. I am not sure about the tooth fairy. Granny says: if Santa Claus can creep about in the night, so could the tooth fairy. It will be winter soon, now it is so dark in the morning. It might be Tuesday. I hope it is. She usually brings me a present. She has funny skin, with brown spots on it. When she is holding me I pull the skin on the back of her hand, and it is like a balloon a few days after a party, all floppy. She says it is not elastic. I can see it is not an elastic but what is it? It looks like a big worm under her skin. Only it is not.

I can hear my clock ticking, but I cannot see where the hands are now. I wish the bell would start ringing. It is so dark, I cannot even see the alphabet which goes round my room. I can remember what most of the pictures are, and the shapes of the letters. When I can put everything together, then I will be able to read for myself. Then I will find out everything. Every letter has a sound, and you put the sounds together to make the words. I keep trying, but mostly the letters fall into bits, and I am left with nothing. But I can do my name, which is easypeasy. I can do it without copying.

10

It is winter now. Mostly, we stay indoors, and get up in the dark. We are doing a play for Christmas, and I am going to be a tree. I do not have any words to say, which is not fair. I want to make some up, but Barbara says trees do not talk. I think trees do, only a different sort of language, so we do not understand what they are saying. Barbara says nonsense, then she says: Anna, don't argue. But I am only trying to *explain*. I am crying. I do not want to be a tree now. Simon is going to be a shepherd, he has lots of words, but he gets them wrong. I would remember. I can remember lots of rhymes, and poems. I can even remember what Simon is supposed to say. O what a lovely star shining in the sky.

I do not talk to anybody all morning. I just play by myself. Martha keeps coming up to me, but I do not even want to talk to her. Barbara asks if I would like to feed the rabbit, but I know why she is saying that, so I say no, I don't. Everybody puts their hand up, and she lets Jessica do it. I wish I was Jessica: she has such beautiful hair. The rabbit has soft fur to touch: I wish I were stroking him.

Barbara says my painting is very good. She holds it up to the class. Everybody looks. I forget I am not going to talk to her and say: could I be an evergreen? What? she says, looking down at me, as though she had forgotten all about it. So I tell her: I don't mind being a tree, if I can be an evergreen. Being deciduous is horrid, now it is winter, their branches look ugly with no leaves on. Barbara looks surprised, but says all right, I can certainly be an evergreen. I jump up and down. So I can wear green, which is almost my favourite colour? Yes, she says, so long as you do not jump up and down. Trees have to stand still. I've got an even better idea, I say, now that Barbara and I are talking to each other again. Could I be a Christmas tree? With lights on? No, she says, no lights. But she is going to let me say some words, very quietly.

Evergreen is a pretty word, but deciduous is ugly. It makes me think of mushy leaves lying on the muddy grass in the park, and big black birds going cawcaw in the wind. Green is very pretty, and Mummy is making me a costume. I will have leaves hanging off my arms, and sewn on to the skirt. This is

25

so exciting, I begin rushing up and down the room. Anna is going mad, she says. When boys get excited they are called boisterous. That's what Simon's mummy says he is. And that he is a terror. Which is being like Martha's dog, who gets excited if you play ball with him, and barks a lot.

Simon sometimes pretends to be a dog, and growls. And pretends to bite people: only he really bit his baby brother, and so he got told off. I would like a puppy, but she says no, not with the new baby coming. I would rather have a puppy than the new baby. I think everything will be horrid when he is born. Everybody will say aah, isn't he sweet, and nobody will look at me. But a puppy is sweet too. All baby animals are sweet, but a baby cannot talk, it just screams a lot, and needs looking after too much. Simon wants a tyrannosaurus rex, a really big one, to stand on his shelf. He already has a brontosaurus and an ichthyosaurus. Simon loves dinosaurs so much, he has a book about them, and so I know all their names too. Dinosaurs are not just dead, they are extinct, so you have to go and look at them in the museum. Daddy took me to the museum, and I knew all their names. Daddy did not, he had to read the labels, or I told him. If there were no books, and no museums, nobody would know about them, which would be silly. And Simon would be very bored, I think.

It is winter, but it is still not snowing. I wish it would snow. I expect it will begin snowing on Christmas Eve, that is when it usually does, in all the story books, and in the films. And children watching from the windows, as big, fluffy bits of snow fall down, and all the world goes white and quiet. Silent night. And perhaps the star shining up in the big black sky. Where the reindeer bells will ring. Magic happens in the dark, when you are not looking. It is dark a lot in winter, which is why there is so much magic. Only it can be scary too. Dreams happen in the dark, and often they are frightening. I dreamt a witch was chasing me in the night, and she put me into a box and turned me into a bird. Abracadabra, she said. If you pull a funny face or cross your eyes, and then the clock strikes, you might be like that for good. But mostly it is the dark. Granny took me to the theatre, and there was a witch, and everything suddenly went dark and there was a very loud noise, and when the lights went on everybody had got turned into animals. They did look funny. I expect Simon would have turned into a dog, into a yappy terror. So when I hear things in the dark I get out of bed to where the lights are still on, and grownups talking as though everything is all right. It is just a story, she said, when I told her about the witch, but I do not know how you can tell, and perhaps grownups do not know either, not always.

Things turn into other things when the light is off. When I can see everything I know what it is. This is my rocking horse, this is my cupboard. I know what everything is called, and when you know that, you know what it is. A is for apple, Z is for zebra, all the letters, all the little pictures running round my room. There is the window, here is the door. We put everything where it belongs: my books on the book-shelf, with the bookends which look like owls, only they are made of wood. When Ellen puts things in the wrong place I get cross. No, I say, and put it where it is supposed to go. Helen sleeps in my bed, so does Teddy. Toto stays down by my feet, and Babar sits on top of the chest of drawers. Just so.

But as soon as she switches the light off, things start moving about, changing. I try to shut my eyes tight. If I do not I see things, and I do not know what they are. Dark shapes, with no names. Peculiar shadows, and I do not know how they got where they are. I keep looking, and the harder I look the less I know about it. What is it? What will it do? I listen, and hear noises too, bumping and creaking, or the wind rattling the window. The more I listen, the more I hear, and then it is not the wind at all. Now it is living, with eyes, and ears, and a mouth. The mouth is breathing, puffing, trying to get in. If it has arms it could grab hold of me, and do things.

Daddy turns the light on, and suddenly everything is what it was before. Here is the cupboard, there is the shelf. I know what everything is called, and what it is for. Daddy says everything is the same in the dark, it just looks different. Things cannot turn into other things. But tadpoles turn into frogs. And caterpillars turn into butterflies. You do not always need magic, even. What is more, he says, sitting on the edge of the bed, with the yellow light shining all round the room, A for apple, Z for zebra, there are no witches. What do you mean? I ask. They do not exist, he says, picking up Toto. I ask him if they are extinct, but he says no, people just thought there were witches, because they were frightened in the dark. I am frightened in the dark, so I do think there are witches, sometimes. Dorothy met a witch, I say, whilst Daddy is holding Toto. Who is Dorothy? he asks, so I tell him. But that's just a story he says, and turns out the light.

I make sure the door is not shut. There is the cupboard, here is the shelf. If there is no such thing as a witch, what is the word doing? Why is it flying about in the night on a broomstick? I cannot think of the answer. Where is the cupboard, where is the shelf? I shut my eyes tight, to keep out the dark shadows.

I feel safe in my room, when I can see everything. But in the dark I do not know what everything is, especially if I am not sleeping in my own room, but even if I am I do not know what the dark shapes are. I keep looking at something black and I do not know what it is. I keep looking at it. It is not moving, so it will not touch me. Perhaps it will do something if I shut my eyes. No. I tell myself I am being silly. In the morning it is just a box. Another morning it was the wooden thing for drying my clothes. Mummy says it is a clothes horse, but Ellen says it is a spider. They argue about it. I say they are both silly, it does not look like a spider or a horse. A horse has four legs and a spider has lots more, but this thing does not have any at all. It is just a thing for drying clothes. Ellen says a spider folds up and down, not sideways. Spiders fold up in the bath when you turn the tap on,

pretending to be dead. I pretend to be dead sometimes, just for a joke. I lie very still, trying not to
blink. Now I am pretending to be asleep, but I cannot
stop thinking. I keep talking in my head. I know how
to draw spiders. I showed Ellen, drawing one in the
air. Where? she said. There, I said, doing it again. It's
just pretend, silly. I can't see it, she said, but I knew
she really could. When the baby is born, he will not
be able to talk. Not even to himself. So he will sleep
mostly. I am sleeping. I am a baby. It is dark, it is
warm. I am going. Going to.

II

It is New Year. I do not know why they call it that: it
looks just like the old one. Actually, it looks more like
the old than it did when it really was. Most of the
needles have dropped off our Christmas tree, so it
was deciduous all along. Grownups keep lying. I feel
difficult. There was a bit of snow, but it got all dirty,
and now it is just messing everything up. I feel
difficult, so I lie on the floor, getting needles stuck in
my clothes. They prick my skin, and are not even
green now, just dirty brown. I do not know what I
want, only that I am not getting it. All my new toys
are old now, and boring. I want to keep the tree, even
if it is not evergreen. There are still lots of needles,
perhaps they will stay on. We could stick them. But
Daddy says the tree has to go. It was an evergreen,

but it has no roots. It is dead. As it has no roots, he says, it can't drink any water, so it has gone all dry. This is interesting. I get up off the floor. Show me, I say. So he lifts it out of the pot and needles start falling all over me. I touch the bottom, where there is nothing. My finger goes round and round. It has been cut, he says, cut down in the forest.

We put all the pretty things in a box. For next year, he says. I do not want to put them away, so I ask him: when is next year? Well, this year, actually, he says, but first we have to have spring, and summer, and autumn. This is boring. If we had a tree with roots, we could plant it in the garden. Mummy is upstairs with the baby, which is even more boring. He sleeps a lot, and she is tired, mostly. I think he was a bad idea. He looks funny, all red and wrinkly. I would rather have had a puppy, they look really sweet, and you can play with them. If I try to play with Harry, she tells me no, you will wake him up, make him cry. I try talking to him, and he looks at me. If I am by myself I try hitting him. He cries a lot anyway.

Could we plant a Christmas tree with roots? Could we buy it now? But he is not listening. When he is not listening properly it goes in one ear and out the other. This happens quite often when he is busy. He is busy now, throwing the tree out into the street. There is a bit of silver left at the top, so I follow him out to get it off. The bit with no roots in it is sticking up into the air. The trunk, he says. Elephants have trunks, so do trees. How very funny. Hello elephant tree, I say. This is a joke.

Actually, the tree is just rubbish now. It is lying out

in the street, getting dirty. After it has been lying out all night I do not want it back. It was out there yesterday: I can see it from the window today. What is today? I ask Ellen. Monday, she says. Is Monday a special day? No, she says. Daddy is not here. Mummy is taking Harry to the doctor. Everybody is in a hurry. It is grey and cold, nobody is coming to visit us, and the tree is still lying by the dustbin, looking very deciduous. It is horrid. Monday is not much good either. Ellen is in a bad mood, telling me to put on what she tells me to, not what I want to wear. Mummy hears, and tells me to do as I am told. No arguing. Everything is rushing along, all the cars, nobody is stopping for anything. The clouds are rushing along up above the street. It is going to rain soon. Barbara makes us do numbers, which is boring. It is boring because it is difficult, and I do not know the answers. Barbara has a cold, so she says nubbers, which is funny. She is a funny colour, like the tree by the dustbin, only light, not dark. She yells at Simon, but starts coughing. I get her a drink of water when she asks me. Trees drink from the bottom, but people do it from the top. Barbara says after Monday comes Tuesday, which is not a special day either. She writes up the days on the blackboard, but I cannot read them yet. Only the first letter. M. T. There are too many ordinary days, and they go on for ages. I count them, but give up. I am not very good at counting. Barbara says no day is ordinary, and that Monday is called after the moon. Moonday. I can't see the moon, I say. Sunday is called after the sun then, says Jessica. And adds: when it is sunny people don't go to work, they sit in the garden or go for a picnic. Sunday is not for working. And Friday is for frying fish, shouts Simon, jumping up and down. Sit down, says Barbara, coughing. You must not talk without putting your hand up. If everybody talks at once nobody can hear anything. Well, she says, lots of people do eat fish on Friday, but that is because they are Catholics. Friday is called after a goddess whose name was Freya. Barbara is looking very ill, she can hardly say anything for coughing, but now everybody is asking questions, and all at once. What's Catholic? What is a goddess? This is exciting. I do not want to do numbers. I want to hear about everything, but Barbara is not in the mood, she wants us to add up. I want to know what a goddess looks like: does she wear some sort of crown? Where do goddesses live? Roger says Catholics shoot people, but not always. His auntie lives next door to some and they are very nice, they gave him a lollipop. Emily says lollipops are bad for your teeth. Barbara says quiet! Very loudly, and bangs on the blackboard.

We do numbers. Johnny has three apples but he gives one to Benjamin. Johnny has ten pennies but buys a balloon. Everybody has to sit down and think, and it is confusing. I get it wrong, and I do not know why. When I do not know why I would rather do something else, but Barbara says no. I look out of the window and the day is grey. No moon. Just grey, an ordinary day.

When I get back it is still Monday. I am told to tidy up my playroom. I am told not to disturb the baby, who is sleeping. It is Ellen's afternoon off. There is

33

nothing much to do. Daddy is not here, Mummy is, but isn't. She is not listening, she is not looking, she is not doing much. She will not play with me. Not now, she says. She is putting her feet up, looking out of the window. I do not know why: nothing is happening out in the street. I hit her, but not hard, not so as it could hurt. Oh God, she says, not looking at me. I do not know why, what I did wrong. If only she would *say*. But she is just looking out of the window.

12

My name is Anna Elizabeth Hart, and I am eight and a quarter. I live at forty-nine Fortescue Avenue, which is in England, which is a little blob on the map. I live with my mother and my father and my brother Harry. Harry does not go to school yet, and says baby words like bow-wow for dog. I can read properly, by myself. It is like learning to walk: first you have to go very slowly, stopping all the time. Then you keep going, except when there is a difficult word. Mostly, I know what grownups are saying. If they do not want me to know what they are saying they speak French. When I am bigger I am going to learn French too. Then I will know everything.

I want to know everything very much. When I have read all the books in the library, then I will know everything. The library is in Springfield Road.

Springfield Road and our road are both in London, which is the capital of England, which is an island. Although it looks like a blob on our map it is really big. Other countries are bigger, but our country is right in the middle of the entire world. Lots of people try to speak English, but they do not speak it properly. Jamila, in our class, could not, but I helped her. Her parents do not have much money, so their house is not very nice. I pretend not to notice, and I do not say anything about it. It is rude to talk about it. Her mother knows hardly any English, so it is difficult to talk to her, but she smiles a lot and gives us funny food for tea. I pretend to like it. It is rude not to eat food, or leave bits on your plate. So now I say I am not hungry. Mostly, I ask Jamila to come to my house. She likes coming, and she likes our food. She even likes Harry, who is boisterous.

Jamila says I am very lucky to live in such a nice house. She thinks we are rich, because of our house. We have four bedrooms and a garage. But we are not, not really. I asked my mother if we were rich and she said no, just average. I am not sure what average means. My mother told me it means sort of ordinary, but my teacher says it is when you add a big number to a small number and then divide it in two. So average is having three bedrooms, because four and two make six and half of six is three. Jamila's family have to squash everybody into two tiny bedrooms, where there is no room to play. I feel sorry for Jamila. I gave her my bracelet. My mother says she knows people who have eight bedrooms, and not to worry about it. Jamila is happy, and that is what counts. What counts, she says, is learning things at school.

I go to school every day now, and stay in the afternoon. I can read quite fast now, and know most of the words. When I do not know, I ask the teacher. Often I can guess, even if I have not seen it before, but some words do not look as they should. Now I can read I will be able to learn the truth about everything. When I was young I used to believe some really silly things. I thought there were witches, and I believed in Father Christmas. Harry is so young he still believes in him, and I am not allowed to tell him. I remember once I heard Mummy saying that Mrs Watson dyed her roots, and I kept looking at her feet when she came round, because I thought she had roots like a tree. Now everything is clear, and if it is not I just ask.

I quite like doing sums, but numbers do not do much. Reading is more fun, especially if there are lots of pictures. The pictures tell you what things look like, especially if the story is about the past, when people wore funny clothes and lived in castles. In the past there was still quite a bit of magic, with evil spells and fiery dragons and people falling asleep for a thousand years, so reading about it is exciting. If there were no story books we would not know about it. I like imagining I am a princess in a long gown, riding a horse through a deep forest. In the past there was lots of dark forest, and that is where the magic hid, among the trees. You might meet a talking bird, or a frog who could turn himself into a prince. Or the wolf, of course. Now the trees have all been cut down, and people do not believe in magic any more. I think it just disappeared, like the wolves.

When I am choosing a book I look at the pages first, to see if I think I am going to like it. If the words are all scrunched up together for pages and pages, then I think it might be a bit difficult. It is easier if people in the story talk a lot out loud, and there are white spaces in between. Sometimes they think about things instead and then I get lost. One long word is all right, because you can guess, but if there are lots of them one after another it is not so good. You have to skip that bit. But with some books the words sound so nice that I don't mind if I am not sure exactly what they mean. It is like going into a beautiful world where everybody sings instead of just saying things, and I can listen for ever and not mind what it is about. Just listening makes you know what it is about, so you do not have to worry. When things rhyme words are like that, or if they are very old. I pray thee, Rosalind, sweet my coz, be merry. It is a lot better than saying cheer up, can't you. I wish I could change my name to Rosalind. I pretend the park is the Forest of Arden, but Jessica would not be Celia. She thought it was a soppy game, and that the words I tried to make her say were stupid. She is no good when it comes to imagining things. This forest where Rosalind and the other girl are walking about is extremely magic. You can tell by the way people talk. It is as though they have golden tongues, and as they speak everything around them turns to gold too, so everything is shining and gleaming. It is very strange, but some-how not strange at all when you are in it. When I am in it I do not want to come out. It is as though the birds singing in the trees could speak, are speaking, and the whole world were part of the conversation. So I do not mind if I do not understand every word, or not quite. Verily, truly. By my troth. I prithee. I think there are deer in this forest, lurking gently behind ancient trees. The forest floor is mossy, and there are poems stuck on most of the trees, as though it was a really good treasure hunt. Only marvellous. That's it: marvellous. Magic is just tricks. This is something else. It will not go away. I can always find it.

13

I love nonsense. It is funny, and makes me laugh. It makes me laugh because I know it is nonsense, even if it sounds as though it might not be. I even have a book of nonsense. Daddy can do a trick which makes two and two come out to five, when everybody knows that, really, two and two make four. I do not know how it works. In our house we have some pictures of buildings with funny staircases which do not go anywhere, even though they look all right. I do not know what makes them do that either. I keep trying. As I was going up the stair, I met a man who wasn't there. He wasn't there again today. I wish, I wish he'd go away. This is funny. But then I think, I know just what it means, so it does make sense. It could have been a ghost. Even now, when the light is off, I see things which aren't really there.

14

I am not speaking to Rebecca, and she is not speaking to me. During the morning break we just pulled faces. She stuck her tongue out, and pretended to be very nice to Martha. I pretended not to notice, and kept turning my back on her. I was playing with Jamila, who did not know what was really going on. When we had our lunch I sat with Martha, but I was thinking about Rebecca. I was wondering what she would do. Not speaking is hard work, if it is somebody you know. If you do not know them you are not supposed to speak to them anyhow. Especially if they are grownup. I wish Rebecca did not exist. She is horrid. She is stuck up. First she says I am her best friend, now she says I am not. I never wanted to be her best friend anyhow. I think she is beastly. She is a liar too. She says her father is very important, that he tells people what to do who are on television, but I do not think she is telling the truth. She is always boasting. She says her uncle has a swimming pool, and she goes there at weekends. And that she has a necklace made of real gold. My mother says it is rude to boast, especially about having things which other people might not be able to afford.

I never say anything to Jamila. It is embarrassing, when I go to her house.

Now we are going home. Rebecca watches me as I get my things. I pretend not to see her.

Miss Hoity Toity.

Hoity Toity yourself.

Miss Toffee Nose.

You're a Toffee Nose.

You think you're so special.

So do you.

I do not.

You do.

Miss Clever Dick.

I am not.

Yes you are.

Sticks and stones may break my bones, but silly words can't hurt me.

Why are you crying then?

I'm not.

Cry-baby.

Shut up. You smell, anyhow.

Who says?

Everybody.

See if I care.

Don't care was made to care.

You're just making it up.

No I'm not.

Martha says you often make things up.

Liar!

Yes she does. She says she doesn't like you any more, and she's going to be my friend.

You're lying.

I'm not.

I don't believe you.

See if I care.

Martha wouldn't say that.

Wouldn't she just!

Then she's lying too.

I hate everything and everybody. I do not want to go to school, ever again. I am never going to school, ever again. When I get to my house I go straight up to my room and shut the door. No, I say through the door, I do not want any tea. Go away.

What's eating you? she says.

Nobody's eating me, I say. Go away.

15

I go to school.

The words are put in little boxes on the blackboard. I am the subject, school is the object, go is the verb. The verb is a doing word, and every sentence must have a verb in it, otherwise it is not a proper sentence. The subject is doing whatever the verb says, and is the most important bit of the sentence, which is why the word which is the subject usually comes right at the beginning. Often the subject is doing something to the object, and the verb links them together. The teacher draws an arc across the blackboard. Johnny eats his apple. Jessica strokes the cat. Two more arcs.

Simon puts his hand up. What am I doing to the school?

Disrupting it, usually, replies the teacher. Then she goes on: Going to it is the answer.

I kiss Alison, Simon whispers across the gangway, to Mark, so the entire class can hear him. Alison is an object.

Alison objects, adds Mark, and both start to giggle loudly.

The teacher throws a stub of chalk at Simon. It lands somewhere at the back of the room. She takes a fresh chalk and draws a line, short and sharp after 'I' in the first sentence.

Subject, she says. Then draws a dismissive ring round the rest of the sentence: Predicate.

I is all by itself. Going to school looks like an afterthought, trailing along. Johnny has no apple, Jessica and her cat inhabit separate worlds. A new sentence goes up: My father wears a grey hat. Miss Jenkins puts a ring round 'grey'.

What kind of word is 'grey'? she asks.

Martha puts her hand up, timidly.

A colour word?

Martha's voice is grey. When she says something out loud she speaks hesitantly. You can hear that she thinks she is probably wrong.

That's not bad, Miss Jenkins says encouragingly,

sounding a bit surprised. Grey is what we call an adjective, a descriptive word.

Jessica and the cat vanish in a whitish cloud to make room for this new word: adjective. I look at it, but see nothing.

Now, continues Miss Jenkins relentlessly, striding to and fro, rather as a tiger might do in its cage: Can anyone give me some more adjectives?

Blue, shouts Simon, not bothering to put his hand up.

This is the beginning of a noisy chorus. Red, yellow, pink, every colour in the paintbox, a rainbow arching through the lead-grey air.

Miss Jenkins waits for the hubbub to subside, she pats her hands on the air as though it was a big, excited dog jumping up and down.

Not just colours. What other descriptive words can you think of?

Big.

That's right.

Small.

Yes.

Fat.

Skinny.

Funny.

Silly.

Miss Jenkins turns to the blackboard, rubs out a word, puts in a new one. My father is wearing an old grey hat. Now: My father is wearing a shabby old hat. I do not know why, but my father is beginning to change too. I feel sorry for him.

Now, give me a descriptive word for 'father'.

43

Everybody is shouting: Poor.

My, I am being told, is a possessive pronoun. This is boring. Pronouns and prepositions seem to be just bits stuck in sentences that nobody thinks about much, not ordinarily. I do not want to think about them now. Through the window I see a fluffy cloud passing. Where is it going to? Where did it come from? Why is it up there? How does it come about? I feel I would like to float up in the sky on a cloud.

Anna!

Miss Jenkins is talking to me, looking straight at me. I think she knows I was not listening, saw me gazing out of the window.

As I was saying and, in case you did not hear me, I will say just one more time: a verb can be either active or passive. Would you, if you can bear to concentrate on the subject in hand, give us an example?

I am being asked a question, and I do not know the answer. I am being put on the spot. She is only picking on me because she saw I was not paying attention. I am being victimised, made fun of, made to look stupid.

You are being taught, Anna Hart. What are you being taught?

I am being taught grammar.

Correct. And would you, at a guess, say that this, in your present state of mind, is an active or passive process?

I do not answer.

Anyone?

Luckily, nobody else is sufficiently sure, or brave enough, to say anything, so I can stop feeling stupid.

Her eye wanders far off, here, there. Everybody sits very still, as though she was a bird of prey about to strike.

You are being taught.

The apple has been eaten.

The hat is being worn.

The cat is being kicked.

We are being lashed by her tongue as she paces to and fro, banging a ruler for emphasis.

Who is doing what to whom?

Simon mutters: You are doing this to us. Miss Jenkins blinks at him briefly, then continues.

Is the apple doing anything? The hat? The cat?

Suffering, I think, squealing, running off.

No. But in each case the noun apple, hat, cat, is clearly the subject of the sentence. It stands at the beginning of the sentence, and no other noun is present. Even if there were one, we could still turn everything round: The cat is being kicked by some-body. We turn it round.

Jessica has her hand up: I don't think that's fair.

What isn't?

Miss Jenkins speaks kindly now, as though she had run out of breath.

Well, turning it round like that, it sounds as if it was the cat's fault.

I don't quite follow.

If you turn it round, it feels as if the cat was doing it to itself, if you see what I mean. Even if you do add 'by somebody' right at the end.

You've lost me.

I mean, as if the cat was asking for it. As if it was just there to be kicked in the first place.

Jessica and Miss Jenkins are looking thoughtfully at each other. Miss Jenkins has stopped teaching, is standing still for a moment. There is something about Jessica now, which makes the teacher listen, as she does not usually do.

You mean, the apple is there to be eaten? The hat to be worn?

Yes, whispers Jessica.

And the cat to be kicked.

Yes.

Miss Jenkins nods, but says nothing. This is unusual. She walks to the window and looks out at the clouds. She lets them float for a moment in her eyes. When she turns her voice has changed.

Jessica has made a very important point. The way we put things matters, more than we realise. I want you to think about how you use words. As it happens, the word 'passive' comes from the Latin verb meaning to suffer, so the passive tense has always had that underlying connotation.

I do not know what 'connotation' means. Nobody has taught us anything about Latin, but I know it is a dead language, and that nobody speaks it now, not even at school. I do not know what is wrong with Miss Jenkins: she is talking to us as though I and Jessica and Simon and Martha were really her equals, and she never usually does that.

I sit very still. Everybody sits very still. I am holding my breath, it is so thrilling.

Part Two

1

Anna!

Pretend not to hear. I am not Anna. I do not know whether I have a label, or what it will be, ought to be. Perhaps Anna will do, after all, but I will not be who they think I am. Not Anny-panny, not my child.

Anna!

Pretend to be stone deaf. I am impervious to sounds. I pull up my drawbridge, lie hiding in my fortress, behind walls of stone. Defiance, that is my watchword.

Do I have to come up?

God, this is tiresome. My eyes turn back to the page, trying to shut out the sound. The desire of the moth for the star. Far, far from here. If I could fly through the window, vanish.

Her steps plonk plonk on the stair. Solid, intrusive. Go away, can't you? No such luck. O that her too too solid flesh would melt.

Anna, open this door.

Her hand trying the door handle, her breath on the far side of the wood, in and out, puffing a bit. Disgusting.

I unlock it. Knowing what to expect, I do not look at her.

The state of this room!

It's my room.

Nevertheless, you could tidy up a bit.

It is not my room, not really. It is the room in their house which I am permitted to occupy, on sufferance. They never let me forget it.

All right. I will, later, when I've finished this.

I seem to have heard that before.

Do you want me to fail my exams?

Of course not.

Well then . . .

Please yourself.

Thanks. I will.

Though how you can live in this mess beats me. Just bring those dirty cups down.

All right, all right. Is that all you came up for?

No. Lunch is on the table.

I'm not hungry.

You'll eat lunch with the rest of us.

Harry is already stuffing it in. My father is standing up, carving, speaking to my mother. Nobody looks up. I do not know why I bother. A heavy odour of food, sickening. Nobody looks towards me as I sit down. I might just as well not be here. The smell of food makes me feel sick. A pool of blood oozing on to the meat platter. Yuck. My breasts are disgusting, so is the odour of blood. I keep my legs tight together, trying not to smell it. My father is being boring, going on and on about somebody in his office.

I look down at a bit of dead sheep on my plate, oozing bloody juice. Although it is utterly disgusting, I am hungry. I cannot deny it. The smell sets my mouth watering, that is the worst of it. I resent being put in this ludicrous position. Human beings are barbaric.

Harry stops wolfing his food for a moment to tell us a joke he heard at school. This term, all his jokes are about elephants. Mostly very silly. This one is silly too. But I am fond of Harry, nevertheless. He is just a boy. Boisterous. So full of himself, he might just burst.

Don't talk with your mouth full, says my mother, after she has duly laughed at his joke. She always says this, but Harry always goes on doing it. He has so much to say. Mashed potato falls out of his mouth. Yuck.

A bit more carcass?

My father is looking in my direction, mockingly. Balancing a portion of dead meat on his carving knife.

Dead sheep, says Harry. Dead dog.

Harry! Now my mother's disapproval is real: she sounds shocked.

My father is still holding the portion of roast meat towards me.

Very funny, I say in my most sarcastic voice, whilst I hold out my plate.

Only teasing, says my mother, patting my arm. You stick to your principles.

Hardly, says my father. It's not as though she practises what she preaches.

I will not take part in this conversation. I look

down at my plate and say nothing, eating slowly. I would so much prefer to eat in my room, with the door shut, but she will not permit it.

Lost your tongue?

The food sticks in my throat, which is constricting. I will not speak, I will not cry.

She swallowed it by mistake, says Harry, and is overcome by his own witticism.

I will not have sulking during meals, says my father firmly. He sits at the head of the table, lording over us. Pater familias.

This is a family, says my mother, who sits at the bottom, serving vegetables. I do not ask much, except that we eat together. Except that when we do meet to eat, we converse civilly.

Her voice is chilly. I am the culprit now, but not. The threat of disruption is elsewhere, unseen, in the atmosphere, shifting things. All things held like a web, swaying precariously in a sudden gust of wind. My mother a spider, trying hard to hold it firm.

Meet to eat, says Harry. Eat to meet.

Nobody laughs. He is the only one not to feel the tension. My mother is shifting her shoulders, bridling. A recent mannerism I do not know how to interpret. I feel it has nothing to do with me, whatever I do.

Meat to eat, says Harry, pointing to the bloody scraps still on the dish. Get it?

Very clever, my father says coldly. Now shut up.

Harry looks crestfallen, ready to cry. My mother looks accusingly at my father, strokes Harry's head, leans forward to kiss him.

Sarcasm is the lowest form of wit, I mutter.

What's that you said?

You heard.

Go to your room.

Thanks. It'll be a pleasure.

2

I did not ask to be born. I did not ask for any of this, and now I am expected to show gratitude. For what, exactly? For the enormous favour of being brought into the world, into this stupid house. If my mother had me, which I am beginning to doubt – after all, I have nothing in common with them – if she did indeed give birth to me it was to satisfy her own whim. My feelings did not come into it. The fact that the world is full of pollution, that I must live under the constant threat of extinction from too much traffic, lack of air, poisoned water, this unpromising destiny did not even enter her head when she thought about having a baby, a sweet little thing, to dress up, coo to, much like buying a puppy. A dog who must perform tricks for his supper, sit up and beg, obey commands. I will not, not now.

Something is happening to me, and it is frightening. I do not really know who I am. I have nothing in common with them, and to say that I am Anna Hart tells me nothing. I am Hart because that is my father's surname. He is insensitive, authoritarian, and I detest him when he will not listen. Not listening is his way of showing who is boss.

When I shut myself in my room, I think about who I might be. Or who I am becoming. I am growing, outgrowing Fortescue Avenue, which is ridiculous and petty. It is a mystery to me that neither of my supposed parents can perceive just how petty their day-to-day lives seem, the sheer futility, mind-bogglingly crass. Tidy your room, mow the lawn, turn the music down. Don't shout, give me any of your lip, don't answer back, but speak when you're spoken to. My life to me a prison is.

Last month I read a story about a boy who was brought up in a London slum, but at the end it was revealed that he was really the grandson of a rich and benevolent merchant. Great was the rejoicing in his handsome mansion when the boy was found! His mother had died in the poorhouse, but the boy, though cruelly used, had always shown a refinement and sensitivity not to be expected in a product of the lower orders. Though poor, he showed an endearing honesty, a frank and open countenance, signifying the truth of his breeding.

I remember a story about an earl's daughter who was stolen by gipsies at birth, and whose beauty caught the eye of the young son of the manor when she reached the age of eighteen. After conversing with her on sundry occasions, the handsome youth understood that she could never be prey to an ordinary seduction, and any hint of using his *droit de seigneur* filled him, he knew not why, with unaccustomed shame. Although simply attired, her modesty of demeanour, the grace with which she carried out the humble tasks which daily fell to her lot, could not but strike a deep chord in his heart. The inexplicable shame, *honte* is the word, which had suffused him, was a mystery no longer when it was unexpectedly revealed that this was his long-lost sister Isabelle, stolen from her cradle eighteen years ago. The gipsies, having avoided the area for many years, now deemed it safe to return. But they had reckoned without the small birthmark, shaped like a strawberry, on the maiden's left shoulder. As she was bathing by the river, etcetera, the young *seigneur* watching secretly from behind some bushes, *voyeur* is the word, he instantly recognised his beloved sister. The old earl was at first doubtful but, her identity being confirmed with tears of joy by the old *nourrice*, who had never ceased to blame herself for the abduction of the child, Isabelle took up her rightful place within the castle, the *château dans le forêt*, and was renowned ever after for her acts of charity to the poor, and a particular kindness to travelling people. None were turned away empty-handed.

This was in olden days. But mix-ups continue. Only the other day there was a programme about two babies who were accidentally switched at birth in the hospital, and it took thirteen years for the truth to come out. Neither of the girls wanted to go back to their real parents. Frankly, there was not much to choose between them, or their suburban houses, so why bother? I could see their point of view. And all the hassle of changing schools, and trying to make new friends. It could be really boring. But I do not think my real parents would live in just any old suburban house. I doubt whether they could possibly be ordinary, so their house would also be extraordinary, or at least unusual. I think they would be artists, with wonderful pictures on every wall, or be very famous in the literary world, with lots of fascinating conversation at every meal, and I would listen, and not find it boring, and nobody would mind if I brought a book to the table, they would think it quite normal. Only I wouldn't, because they would always have such interesting things to discuss.

3

I do not know who I am from moment to moment. I try out different hair styles in the mirror, pull faces, look for an answer in the reflection of my eyes. Which are dark, solemn, giving nothing away. Hello Anna, I say, but she does not appear to know me. Or rather, she does not seem to recognise herself when I say Anna. I try another tack. Hello Drusilla. Unexpectedly, she starts smiling, and this changes her utterly. She is lit up from within, eyes shining, every feature somehow different. Mobility is the word. It suits her. And a spark of mischief. Drusilla Hart, distinguished author, with her hair up and long dangly earrings, and eye shadow. I am experimenting with eye shadow, but I have to take it off before I go downstairs. She doesn't mind, but he plays the heavy father. So boring.

Yes. I think I might change my name to Drusilla eventually. You can call yourself what you like once you are grown up, and nobody can stop you, not even your parents. Trust them to choose a boring name like Anna. Just the sort of thing people like them would do. Dru-sil-la. I pout my mouth in a *moue*, and lift my eyebrows in a manner suggestive of arch sophistication, slight cynicism. I look down my rather long nose at the little people who live in places like Fortescue Avenue. This is all you can really do with a long nose. Impossible to seem cute, like Jessica. The boys go for her, with her snub nose and short curls. Everything about her bounces now. Bottom, curls, tits. *She* doesn't like me saying tits. When I say my tits hurt she makes me say breasts. I can't think why: that's what everybody else calls them, except when they talk about breast cancer and things like that. Tit cancer would sound a bit odd. Not serious enough, I suppose. And she stops Harry using words like bugger and fuck, even though he obviously hasn't a clue what they mean. He just knows that's the sort of thing boys say. Anna's tits are titchy, he yelled, so why not? She had to laugh. Laughing at my expense has become a family pastime this past year. I am told I have no sense of humour, that I take myself far too seriously.

Nobody else takes me seriously. They persist in thinking I am still their little girl. That is why I have to remove the eye shadow before going downstairs, and lipstick is *streng verboten*. Such a Nazi, my father.

Drusilla Hart, author of provocative and earth-shattering works of art, would undoubtedly wear dark, sultry lipstick, purple or maroon, possibly dye her hair black too. I intend to write a withering exposé of their narrow-minded values, so suburban and bourgeois, when I earn my own living and can do whatever I want, without fear of shocking anybody or getting told off. I think it is so sick, to say nothing of the hypocrisy. It is okay for *him* to read the paper at breakfast and hardly say a word to anybody, but if I bring down Shelley it is quite another matter, antisocial, even though I might have to do it for exams. I told him, it would do his soul a lot more good to read Shelley than the daily rubbish in the newspapers, and I made a point of propping the book open against the marmalade pot. He gave me one of his Gestapo looks and then he started: Life, like a dome of many-coloured glass, stains the white radiance of eternity. You could have knocked me down with a feather, I just sat there looking at him with my jaw dropping. I didn't want to show I was impressed. Well? he said, looking me straight in the eye. Well, what? I whispered, still breathless with the shock of it. Well, just what is it supposed to mean? I never could figure it out.

I might have known it. Philistine. At least, I think that's what I mean. Not sure who the Philistines were, exactly. Insensitive boor, anyhow. I was going to start telling him what I thought it meant, but then I thought better of it. Logic being his thing, he would go on about physics, about light not being white, something on those lines. Just trying to trap me into looking foolish. That's his idea of a meaningful discussion, proving the laws of physics or whatever. Two and two make four, I know what I know, and so forth. Why bother trying to explain? I know exactly what it means, in fact I can see a vision of it in my head, but try telling him . . . He has absolutely no notion of feeling. I expect he never had an emotion in his life, not really. Nothing deep and meaningful, or he would not make fun of poetry. He is terribly literal-minded, that is his problem, looks at everything literally. Funny that literal and literary should mean absolute opposites.

Mum is a bit more sympathetic, which is hardly surprising. It's her subject, after all. But I think she just goes through the motions now, like having to talk to each other at mealtimes. Being a family, she calls it. Well, if this is being a family, I think it is awful. It never used to be like this.

Why should families talk to each other? I say. Dad hasn't talked to his brother for five years.

There are reasons, he mutters.

So?

Stop arguing.

You see, when I do talk, I am told to stop arguing.

Harry chips in: What is the difference between a big black cloud and a lion with toothache?

Quite a lot, I should think, says my father, turning to the financial pages. At weekends the newspaper is conveniently fat, and he reads it through lunch too.

One pours with rain and the other roars with pain, Harry shouts triumphantly. Neither of them are listening.

Eat your lunch before it gets cold, she says.

Haha, I say, in my most hollow voice.

Harry pulls a face across the table. I stick my tongue out.

Children!

But Harry and I are looking at each other, both laughing now. He is only a kid, but we know how to talk to each other.

He is hiding behind his newspaper, and she is watching him. Even when she is pretending to hear Harry out, or asks what I am doing, her eyes suddenly go empty. She is listening for something else, I think. I think she makes such a big deal of family lunch, turning it into a ceremony, talk, talk, talk, because she is listening for something else, and hears nothing.

4

I am listening, trying not to hear. I put my hands over my ears, trying to shut them out. They are utterly disgusting. She is shouting at him, he is not saying much. Growling in an undertone, I cannot distinguish the syllables. She is slamming doors for emphasis, a whirlwind of fury rampaging through the house. I feel sick. The whirlwind is churning up my stomach. It is scary, listening to it. I do not want to hear this. It is scary, I feel as though the walls of the house were shaking and everything might blow away for good. Where is Toto? I want to cuddle something soft. I want everything to turn out right, to follow the yellow brick road. I want to be Dorothy, for everything to turn out right. If I could go on being a little girl, with my hair in bunches, eating her bread and butter like a good girl, and everything turning out right with a goodnight kiss, when the light goes out.

5

I have put a notice, DO NOT DISTURB, on my door. When I am in here, I also put a chair in front of it. Now and then, when she gets fed up with my not answering, she just barges in anyhow, and starts going on about my giving her a hard time. Not saying anything is a good way of defending myself, and I notice that this tactic seems to get under her skin. I just sit there pretending to study, with my head down, and she gets into a lather. It is not my fault, all this. All I ask is to be left to myself, but it is, apparently, too much.

Anna!

The moment I hear it, I sit very still, hardly breathing. I wish for invisibility, for her to find the room empty, just a few things lying about.

Anna!

O that this too too solid flesh could melt. I sit in my smelly fortress, huddling inside it, wishing not to be found. The things of the spirit come first, but she, they, have no notion of this. Shopping, tidying up, dusting. Nag nag nag.

An-na!

I am writing a diary, which I keep hidden under my underwear. I think she snoops around my room when I am at school, if she is not working. In it I put my innermost thoughts. I bare my soul. I need to do this by writing things down, or I would burst. There are things I cannot talk about to anybody, certainly no one in this house. Besides, I often write things down which I do not want anybody else to know. I would die of shame. I saw him looking at me today, and felt myself going hot all over. I could tell what he was thinking. Every time he looks at me I put a special mark in my diary. Only I know what it means. I need to be by myself, to remember. I need to write it down, or I would burst. I feel my soul is outgrowing my body, and I need to find a way of putting it down in words. Sometimes they are not the words that are really going through my head, which are too raw, too embarrassing. So then I try writing a poem instead, about the moon, or rain dripping from the trees, or the weather.

The weather keeps changing, like my mood. That is why it helps to describe it in carefully chosen words. I am changing from hour to hour, and confiding in my diary is necessary. I will keep it in years to come as a record, a testament of how I was, how I felt. Then, if I turn into just another thick-skinned adult, this will remind me, what living should feel like, really, truly.

I am not a child, I am changing. I look in the mirror

and I see it, two eyes looking back at me, dark, soulful. I know he sees this. I catch him looking at me sometimes, and his eyes have the same look, deep, brooding. Without uttering a word. That is how I know. I put DO NOT DISTURB on my door and think about it, each extraordinary moment. I think I will see every second, in my mind's eyes, for ever. But, just in case I turn out like the rest of them, thick-skinned and so forth, I will put it on record now.

6

I am, they tell me, neither fish nor flesh. I am at an in-between stage. I do not fit in. When Harry asks me why a chicken crosses the road I really cannot be bothered to play along with him, though I go through the motions, just to shut him up. As for Mum and Dad, they are not really sure what to do with me either. If I hang around with them they ask: Haven't you any homework? Are you doing something with Clarissa this weekend? If I am doing something with Clarissa, and it might involve getting in after midnight, then the shutter comes down. Out of the question. Eleven at the latest, and so on.

I hardly ever do hang around, and shutting myself in my room is considered unsocial, especially if people are coming round for tea. Then I am expected to show up, to 'put in an appearance', as Mum calls it, or at least 'say hello'. That is about all I do say. I sit there, feeling like a lemon, swinging my legs and watching. If I watch too obviously it is called staring. If I say nothing, I feel stupid. I keep glancing at my watch, wondering when I can decently leave, and whether I should say nothing, or 'excuse me', or make up something to get myself out of the room. Once I said I had to see a man about a dog and Mum was absolutely furious with me, after they had left. I don't see why. I've heard it said lots of times, and I never thought it meant anything in particular, that it was just a way of going without saying something that nobody was interested in hearing anyhow, or that might even be a downright lie. And there is always the danger that if you do tell the truth, like saying you are going out, that it will start off lots of questions, and then you are there for another half hour. The same goes for homework as an excuse: suddenly they want to know about your favourite subject and what you want to be when you grow up.

When it is Grace and Richard coming round I do not mind being there. On the contrary, when I am not passing round teacups or getting more milk I cannot take my eyes off her, she wears such gorgeous clothes, soft and colourful and sort of flowing. We have really good discussions too, about art and politics and why the government is so awful, and she told me where I could buy beads like hers quite cheaply, though they look fabulous and expensive, and she lent me some of her eye shadow to try. But just when it is getting really interesting, and I am arguing with Richard about the nature of good and evil, Dad interrupts coldly and says: Haven't you got something to do,

Anna? And he looks at me in a queer way, hard, his eyes saying: that's enough now, get out.

It was as though I had been hit, suddenly, out of nowhere. I was struck dumb. The words had been tumbling out: it was such fun, so exciting. Suddenly I was cut short, not part of it, nothing. I could not think what to say. So I left the room without uttering a word. I could feel myself beginning to cry. I sat at my desk, sniffing, staring out of the window. I had barricaded the door. I let Harry in for a bit, later, and we played draughts. I stayed upstairs during supper but got myself some bread and cheese after they had left the kitchen.

I did not draw the curtains when it got dark. I sat at the window. The desire of the moth for the star, I repeated. The desire of the moth for the star. I could see several above the dark of the trees.

7

The body has its own language. It was dumb, and now it speaks. I lie in the dark and hear it, the mouth twitching, whispering smutty secrets. I pretend not to hear, but it will go on, on, till I ache. O Mr Pettifer, I whisper, the mouth whispers too, and suddenly I am speaking to him urgently, telling him what I could never tell him in daylight, because of our ages, because of his wife, that I love you, love you, my body is telling you this now, all of it, from head to foot, my mouth is talking so fast now, the words making me giddy, when I hear the words I feel my head spinning, sounds running down the rest of my body. All of it hears, reacts, greedy for more, more of the whispering, in my ear, in his, I know he hears me, I feel it, he is telling me back, everything he could never say, not out loud, beautiful, he says, so so beautiful, and my body is telling him it knows, how much it knows, answering him, reassuring him, nobody need know about us, I tell him, pleading, urging him, nothing shameful if we love each other, nothing. And I do. Oh how I do, says the mouth, the lips, every inch of my burning skin.

8

I feel how the sun caresses my skin. I am wearing shorts, to get my legs brown. I wear a straw hat with a wide brim so the sun will not get in my eyes whilst I am reading. Nor do I want a burnt patch on my nose, which will go an ugly red colour, and then peel. To get the back of my legs the same shade of brown I will have to lie on my tummy, on the blanket I have also brought out, for an hour or two. My legs look good. My arms look good, too, especially in a white shirt.

I am reading in the back garden. When I was a small child I thought this garden was enormous. Now it seems quite small. Cosy though, with trees and hedges to hide us from the neighbours. I expect the ladybird crawling up my forearm thinks this garden is the universe, all of it. My arm a hairy continent. I might write a poem about it. Perhaps it should be an ant, really, to serve my purpose. An ant would be more appropriate. They never look up, or fly off, and are oh so busy negotiating their way through Lilliput, never realising it is only my arm.

I am growing, this garden is shrinking. But if I look up the sky is endless, dizzying. Fortescue Avenue, the universe. A short cut, no need for town, postcode, or country. Look up and feel my soul grow dizzy with it, the ether, ethereal, and unending. The world turning, I, Anna, turning with it. Words begin flying, wispy as bits of cloud. My heart leaps up when I behold. My soul doth. I spin in eternity, looking up, up. I am whirling through emptiness, an atom of nothingness, floating, falling, nothing but gravity pinning me down to earth, to the grass tickling the backs of my knees, my neck. The relativity of everything. I, Anna, the ant crawling through a forest of lawn seemingly without end, myself a continent somnolent in the sun, stretching, feeling, unknown territory to every insect, vast: perilous too. I see a ghostly moon hang in the blue sky, high above Lilliput Avenue, whilst insects whirr and our neighbour is whistling an unknown song.

I sit up. I got a new book out of the library this morning. I have already read several books by this author. I know where I am with him. I read the opening page. 'Mr Brown had lived in the town of ——— all his life. He felt comfortable in it. He knew

67

everybody, and everybody knew him. What is more, they respected him.' No whirling clouds now. You know where you are with this story. No whirling words taking off into the unknown, pulling the ground from under you. I can see the town, I can see Mr Brown. He is rotund, a word which speaks for itself, for the sort of story this is. If he were fat, or overweight, then I would not know what to expect: he might suddenly drop dead of a heart attack. Madeleine's father did. But this Mr Brown, who is rotund, who wears a watch chain across his waistcoat and runs a chemist shop, I know where I am with him, especially as I have read other books by this author. He never lets you down, nothing really beastly happens to nice people. And Mr Brown is a nice character. Balding slightly, with a moustache and wire-rimmed spectacles. I can just see him. Elderly, I think about forty, he has been keeping this shop as long as people can remember, punctually opening his shutters at nine every morning, closing them as the church clock strikes six. A confirmed bachelor, so he could not hurt a fly if he wanted to, never quarrels with anybody. Mr Brown is very fond of his cat, for whom he buys a choice morsel of fresh fish every Friday, as a special treat.

I settle myself into a more comfortable position and wonder whether I should take a peep at the last page, but that is cheating, and might spoil it. I do not think Mr Brown is going to do anything unexpected. That is the point. If anything happens, it will happen to him. Sort of in the passive tense. The fact he is a

68

chemist might be a clue. Poison? No, this is an English story, set in England. If he were living in a small town in France it would be quite a different matter. They do a lot of murdering in the French provinces. As soon as you read the word pharmacy, which is the word they use, you know it is going to be a story involving poison. There is a lot of illicit passion and scheming for money in French provincial life, and the pharmacist usually has something to do with it.

Mr Brown is a character, which means he is consistent. I know where I am with him, just as I know every avenue and crescent and close in this suburb. I feel safe with him. I do not suddenly get scared, feeling a tornado shaking everything. Mr Brown can be relied on, otherwise he would not be a character at all – he would be out of character, and I would stop believing in him. Mr Brown makes me feel safe, in control of things, as he always does the sort of things you expect him to do. Fussy, but kind, he would never get sarcastic when you least expect it, nor vanish for hours on end without giving a reason. The reason would either be obvious, or the author would just tell you, so you could stop worrying about it and get on with the next chapter. You can read him like a book. Well, he is a book. He never has incomprehensible thoughts strung together without proper grammar and full stops, which I find so utterly confusing, especially when you are not told whether something is really happening or is just thoughts. Suddenly, instead of just going along, following the signposts, stops, commas, avenue, high street, market square, you find yourself stumbling over what seems a heap of rubble, chaotic, no way through. Big words piling on top of each other, unfamiliar, or not connecting up properly. Things should join up as they always did, not turn into chaos, a war zone, nothing is as you thought it was, unintelligible, no way through.

This is what I like about this story, all the signposts are where I expect them to be. I can easily read them. No fear of earthquakes, war, or a sudden tornado. Come, say the words, I will take you by the hand, lead you down winding old streets. You will hear the church clock strike punctually on the hour, you will watch Mr Brown, bit of a fuddyduddy, but with his heart in the right place, give cream to his cat on Sunday, on all the other days walking punctually to his chemist's shop, lifting his hat to the ladies. Ping goes the shop door, and Mr Brown gets unusually flustered: it is the headmaster's wife, who is kind to him, her blue eyes have held him spellbound for years. Not that he would ever do anything about it, this secret yearning, this passion which turns him pink as the geraniums in the market square, no. For this is England, this is the town of ———, this is Mr Brown, set in his ways, in his sleepy town, unchanging. Mr Brown would never slam doors so the house shook from top to bottom, or vanish in the middle of lunch, leaving his second chop. No. Mr Brown walks to work through the quiet streets, where nothing much has altered in a hundred years. He would not suddenly drive off in the car, upsetting everybody's plans. I can rely on Mr Brown. I expect he will just grow older, slowly, a little greyer, a bit more rotund by the end. I can turn back and remind myself of how he is exactly, how he was put down in black and white at the beginning. Memory is clear and foggy by turns, distorting, wiping things out. Sun rising and bits of cloud, gigantic figures looming. I can turn back to the beginning if I want to, or flick forward to see how things will turn out. Not enough to spoil things, just enough to know where things are heading. Whether I should expect the ending to be happy or not.

9

Growing up means, I find, doing a lot of pretending, and not saying what you really think. Whenever I say what I really think I get into trouble, and that is just my own family. And you should see how they go on when it is other people, how they say one thing to their faces and the exact opposite behind their backs. Take the Scannells, for example. I heard him say, *not* the Scannells, for heaven's sake, when she told him this morning, and she was apologising, saying she could hardly avoid having them round, and it was not as though they were staying long, just an hour.

So now he is saying how much he had enjoyed the dinner party the other night, when in fact I heard them say how boring it was, the food dreadful, the company worse. Mrs Scannell is hideous. She wears too much lipstick for her age, has nobbly legs with blue veins showing through, and her teeth are ugly. I watch her mouth as she speaks, smiling too much, showing too much tooth. Actually, she really is long in the tooth. I enjoy thinking this is in my head. Saying things, but not out loud. I am not going to say anything, just sit, working my way through the bowl of crisps.

The less people have to say to each other, the harder they try to keep on talking. I think they are scared of stopping. Whenever there is a pause in the conversation my mother hastily starts off a new topic. That story about walking on a grave, she must think it's hers. She and Mrs Scannell are doing most of the work, the men are not saying much. Dad keeps trying to pour more drinks too soon, fiddling with the ice bucket, tossing olives into his mouth. Mr Scannell seems not to be listening at all. He gets up, starts looking at things. First of all he stares at the painting over the fireplace, then he turns his head askew and starts reading the titles of books on the shelves. He pulls out a volume and begins to flick through the pages. Then he actually sits down with it, reading.

I watch Mr Scannell reading. He's probably quite nice, despite his looks. Everybody else is watching him too. His wife keeps throwing furious glances at him, but he doesn't look up. I can't think why they ever got married. Imagining them naked together, I nearly laugh out loud.

Mrs Scannell pulls a packet of cigarettes out of her handbag.

Do you mind if I smoke?

But she has already lit it.

Of course not.

Liar, I think, staring hard at my mother. She avoids looking in my direction, gets up to find an ashtray. Dad has to go to the bottom of the garden every time he stops giving it up. Mum pointedly opens all the windows, very wide, creating a draught. Mrs Scannell, however, seems impervious to the atmosphere. Her back is to the open window. If she feels the cold air blowing in she gives no sign.

Such hypocrites, the lot of them. I will never behave like them when I am their age. It is as though they are acting in a play, and keep forgetting their lines. I have almost got through the crisps, but I know I am not going to get another drink. Perhaps I will just help myself. It is like Mrs Scannell smoking, Dad could hardly stop me with them watching. I did not want to be here, but now it is rather amusing. Mrs Scannell catches my eye, sees me staring at her, and gives me a vague sort of smile. I just go on staring, sphinx-like. This makes her uneasy, I can see. Her eyes shift, then she glances at me again, uncertainly. I go on looking stony-faced, meeting her gaze without blinking. I expect she thinks I am thinking something unpleasant about her, and is trying to guess what it is. I watch her mouth moving, her conspicuous teeth, how she stubs out the cigarette with her predatory talons, angrily. Several rings, red nails. Mutton dressed as lamb, Mum said this morning. I think of a scrawny bird of prey, long neck, all claw and beak, keeping a hold on Mr Scannell.

Mr Scannell has put down the book and is trying to join in the conversation, which is faster now, and louder. But it is hard for him to find a way in. My father and Mrs Scannell both talking at once, everything going swimmingly now the drink has begun to work. But Mr Scannell is stranded, he has missed the boat, sits on the further shore, looking on. I think he is quite sweet really, in a funny sort of way. He could be Mr Brown, the chemist, apart from the whiskers. I bet I could make him fall in love with me, if I tried, with his awful vulture wife. I bet he is hen-pecked, unhappy, ready to begin nursing a secret passion. Shy too, much too shy to be difficult, or do anything.

I begin looking at Mr Scannell. My eyes are soft, dreamy. I am willing him to look at me, my young body, legs showing under my short skirt, unmarked skin, eyes to drown in, milky complexion. It would be fun if I could get him to fall for me, provoke a blush perhaps. That would be one in the eye for Mrs Scannell. Nobody is asking me what I think, nobody is offering me anything to drink. I might not exist. But I do, very much so. I am just beginning, everything is beginning now. I could try it out. I could probably do it, if I set my mind to it.

But it is Mum who is looking at me, hard. I defy her to say something, raising my eyebrows. Instead of speaking, she lowers her eyes to my exposed thighs for a second, then raises them to look back directly into mine. I do nothing, pretend not to understand, lifting both eyebrows and shoulders in query. But she

74

repeats the unspoken signals, too obviously now for me to pretend incomprehension, slightly injured innocence. I pull down my skirt, but not without wriggling my bum vigorously.

10

Metamorphosis.

I am changing. It hurts, but I feel it.

Metaphor.

An ugly duckling turning into a swan. No. An ugly grub into winged creature, ready to fly. Longing to go: but where? Into light, into night. The desire of the moth for the star. Far, far off. Mysterious, unknown. I will fly, fly.

I sit by the window and see the clouds drift high overhead. Who am I now? Anna, I hear, but do not reply. Choosing to hear nothing, only the wind in the trees, light and shadow passing, my own heart beating. I am all things, and nothing, running with water, flying with clouds. Sticky wings, antennae searching blindly.

When is a door not a door? Harry has his head round it.

When it's shut, I answer, annoyed at his bursting in.

NO, he shrieks. When it's ajar. Get it?

A jam jar?

Harry looks nonplussed. I get up, go to the door.

This is a jamb, I say, touching wood.

I don't believe you, says Harry. You're making it up.

No, I'm not. Ask anybody.

I spell the word for him.

Momentarily nonplussed, he listens attentively.

Well, he says, what goes up and down stairs without moving?

Luckily for him, I do not have an inkling.

I am told, triumphantly, that it is a stair carpet.

Harry goes off, loudly, kicking things. Full of himself, just about bursting with it. Whatever he is, batman, superman, deep-sea monster, Harry is still Harry, and knows it. Prick him, he will not puncture, or only for a moment, bouncing back into his skin. Lucky Harry. I feel it hurting, under my skin. Turning. I could cry, but do not know why.

I feel a shadow running across the land, my skin, the water. A darkening. I feel a shudder rippling, fear of the unknown. Rumours of death running through the grass, touching my arm, shaking trees. Shadow on the sun.

The shadow steals across water, revealing unknown, unexpected depths, this lurking profundity. I want to dive down, losing myself in it, but avoid drowning. Losing myself, to find, to find something. This emerging other. If the sun is shining the pool gleams, bright as a mirror. Words go quack quack. Quack quack go the ducks, paddling busily, mothers and babies throwing crumbs. Harry asking why chickens cross the road, not wanting my answer. To and fro, ping pong. But now I feel this shadow creeping, this dumb wind rippling the mirror, disturbing it. I must withdraw, diving into this dark pool where I hear nothing, no ordinary daylight words, no to and fro, lightly, brightly, bouncing off the liquid mirror. How are you? asks the mouth, so the reflection promptly answers: How are you?

No. I must try diving, hear nothing of all this, chitterchatter, begin diving, under, down to where aqueous shadows lurk, spectral, mouthing unfamiliar messages. Where a new self is shaping, I think. Mouthing dumbly like a fish, swimming through the dark, gills for lungs, picking up a new language. Shadow stirring on shadow, gliding through, not knowing which is illusory, a blue-green mood swing only, and which is rock. Hard, ungiving. Metamorphosing into this alien world, mysterious, far from the hard-edged brightness of things, yes or no, objects neatly labelled. Ducks flailing along, webbed feet visible just beneath the surface. Ducks ducking, quacking. A paper boat bobbing, beginning to sink now, absorbing the dark water.

No. It will not do, all this. How to know shadow from substance, subject from object? No neat little boxes, no. Dabbling my fingers, the clear surface shatters, rippling out, wiping my reflection, each familiar image. I must begin plunging, dying fearlessly, to come up breathing deeply with my new lungs.

Part Three

I

The hubbub in the room is rising. I cannot make out individual words, but everybody is talking, talking. I do not know if anyone can hear themselves. I doubt whether they feel sure of being heard. But that is not the point. The point is to speak, to go on speaking with the maximum vivacity, to hold the eye, if not the ear, to keep whirling in the swim of it now, to stay part of it, the words bubbling out, such fun, so much to say, or so many ways of saying it, holding his eye, holding hers, so his eye, hers, will try desperately to lipread, watching the mouth moving if the hubbub drowns out all sound. Not on any account to get swept aside, stranded, as I am standing now, at the edge of it, back to the wall, looking in. Once that happens, once you stand, as I stand, looking in, hearing the hubbub rising but not comprehending a word, no individual thread running audibly through it, worth picking up on, following for a bit, to stand once more at the heart of it, the labyrinth, hubbub, words toing and froing, finding an eye, an ear perhaps, or merely floating off into the night, the dark, the atmosphere; once that happens you are done for. Washed up, stranded. Isolation rapidly leading to speechlessness, the dumb dark hollow swelling, misery. Get back in there, I tell myself, feeling such a fish out of water, gasping in the wrong element.

My thigh touching a small table, a lamp standing on it. Most of the room is in shadow, but the lamp casts a dim ring of light on to the ceiling. Intense light flowing down, spilling on the bright wood, down my silk skirt. Out of it now, the moving whirlpool of sound, unexpectedly stranded, looking in. Not knowing how to rejoin the swim, or whether I even want to. The room is filling up, nowhere to go, a wall of people with their backs to me, hemming me in. I stand, turning into a wallflower, feeling like a lemon and mixing my metaphors to relieve the tedium. Nothing like a bit of knowing irony to save face, a saving grace in this ridiculous, slightly embarrassing situation.

The group standing near me expands to admit newcomers, ignoring me. Apparently invisible, I tell myself that alienation is the only way to be – not that I have much choice just now – thus detaching myself from the herd, this common mob, disdainful of it. Silly, noisy. But really I feel depressed, black melancholy rising, seeping up, up. Soon it will reach my mouth, eyes. I am nobody, nothing.

A shoulder so close to me I can see the texture of his jacket, every thread. The short hairs on the back of his neck, an angry red pimple between earlobe and collar. And then, as laughter explodes like a sudden grenade at its centre, the ring moves outward slightly and the man with the pimple steps backward on to my foot, without noticing, without so much as turning round, with no apology.

This is too much.

Excuse me, I say brusquely, pointedly, pushing my way through the group, who look startled, mouths stopping in mid-sentence, eyebrows rising slightly as they exchange glances. I do not know them, have not been introduced either, so it hardly matters if I push through them. That is the trouble with this party: too many people I do not know, and nobody bothering with introductions.

I head for the drinks table at the far end of the room. It makes me look purposeful. My glass is empty, but I am trying to find someone I know, by now almost anybody would do, just so long as I could hook into the talk, find my way into it, this hubbub, this whirlpool of sound, hear myself speaking and being spoken to, anything would do, who are you, how do you do, toing and froing, gossip, do you know him, have you met her, words, words, their meaning in noise itself, their purpose unspoken. I am here, they scream with delight, making themselves heard through the hubbub, in the thick of it, playing my part, toing and froing, catching a word here, a phrase there, tossing it back with agility, scoring points. Nobody must catch me out, no sudden twist of direction, I am ready for it, no topic too high for me, no word too hard, I will keep it in play. I hear it, pushing through it with my empty glass, she was born in Chiswick, he thinks Ezra Pound misunderstood, they have met at a conference in Edinburgh, Melissa had an abortion last month but didn't want anybody to know, so don't let on I told you. Anything to keep it going.

I pour wine into my empty glass, wondering how much of it I should drink to get in the right mood. Too little, and I will go on standing at the edges, looking in; too much, I could make a fool of myself, or just feel sick. It loosens the tongue but taketh away controul thereof. The high can be followed by a sickening slump into depression. I sip, looking in, at the unknown faces half hidden in shadow, collectively now producing this hubbub, the unmistakable hum signifying a successful party. The doorbell is ringing, latecomers squeeze through the door, the hubbub is a chorus now, of triumph, triumph at being part of it, this successful gathering of whoever is up and coming, popular, worth knowing. Such fun, such excitement, so reassuring too, to be here, not to have been excluded from this successful gathering, getting to know them or, better still, showing that you know them already, smiling gaily at the attempted introduction.

I watch, looking in, not doing what I should be doing, which is to get in there, pick up a thread of conversation, any thread, and see where it leads. Not so different from a children's party really, with no hanging back, refusing to join in. Grownups cajoling, bullying even, the odd cringing child. Come on,

Anna, stop sulking. But I stand, unwilling, hanging back. Clutching my armour of selfhood to me, relinquishing nothing. I, subject, looking with hard eyes. Refusing to join in, chatter, pick up a thread and go with it, even though you know it will lead nowhere, to the moment when you are left standing with a bit of cut string in your hand. Hard luck, Anna, keep trying. Such fun, playing the game. Let us all join in.

Nothing beyond this room but a dark void. I know this, standing on the verge of the party, now in full swing, pouring wine into a bottomless pit of misery. Alice knows it, moving triumphantly through the room, eyes blazing, cheeks on fire, speaking to her guests in turn. Wherever she is, this is the focal point, the maelstrom's eye, where the talk is louder, laughter more shrill. Everybody in her vicinity gets sucked into her spirit, so full of energy, enthusiasm and verve. They feed her with their presence, the admiring glances, responsive laughter, quick words, and so she glows hot instead of dying, feeding them in turn.

Nothing now beyond this room, only a void. I know this, trying to reach the french window standing open to the night. The latecomers know it, coming in from the night, squeezed helplessly in the crush. Beyond light and sound, nothing. Empty city, silent sky, a dim glimmer of stars in the void.

Leaving now is not really an option. I see a few familiar faces on the far side of the room and begin to weave my way through the crush. In the thick of it, I find myself unable to move. Unavoidable eye contact

with a stranger. He is prolonging it, smiling unambiguously.

Quite a party.

Yes.

Do you know most of these people?

No. Hardly anyone. And you?

Not a soul.

So how did you get here?

A friend brought me. Adrian Chadwick. Do you
know him?

No.

He's over there somewhere. Or, at least, he was.

I see.

And you?

What about me?

How did you get here?

Alice invited me.

Who's Alice?

Our hostess. Whose party did you think this was?

Sorry. Stupid of me. Which one is she?

Over there. The girl in red, holding a bottle.
Didn't your friend introduce you?

Afraid not. Suddenly he was gone.

What?

HE JUST WENT OFF. SUDDENLY. I
EXPECT HE GOT SWEPT AWAY.

Oh.

So is she a friend of yours?

Who?

Alice.

Sort of. Alice knows everybody.

So it seems.

I bump into her at lectures, that sort of thing. We're in the same faculty.

Which is?

English. We're both doing History of Literary Criticism, so I see her there every week. A group of us usually have lunch afterwards.

What?

WE LUNCH!

Really? I'm dying for a drink.

They're over there, if you can get through.

How about you?

No thanks.

Are you sure?

Positive.

Your glass is empty.

I've had enough for the moment.

Well, if you're sure. I'll be right back.

I watch him begin to weave his way through the room, then vanish. Well, I let him lightly off the hook, poor fish. Go swim. Though I am dying for a drink, catch me standing here for the next half hour whilst he chats up a tastier morsel elsewhere, out of sight, out of mind, he thinks, with most of the room between us. I know this ruse: getting a drink is the opt out, escaping with minimal fuss. Only a fresher in her first term would take such talk at face value. Perhaps I should go. Perhaps I should get myself a drink: I might meet a familiar face on the way. I see Doreen a few yards off, but have nothing new to say to her since this morning. I think the History of Criticism put him off. No walking to and fro, talking of Michelangelo for him, no. I should, I think, cultivate a lighter touch, party patter, going through the motions ad infinitum, tossing the silly shuttlecock to and fro, whilst the mind wanders off, the eye with it, searching the room for anything that might turn out to be a tastier morsel, exciting, inviting. But I have to start somewhere, find a foothold, common ground, uncommon, anything to set things truly in motion, the possibility of engaging at some point, cogs setting wheels in motion, going somewhere.

I think of leaving, of slipping quietly into the night. I will walk the empty streets under a dark unending sky, my footsteps echoing hollow. Opting for speechlessness, subjectivity. Hearing my own footfalls, my random thoughts. Better than this play-acting. But I must go tactfully. Whether to approach Alice, plead a headache, an essay to finish? Or do nothing, simply go quickly, invisibly? So soon? she will say, disappointed, a touch of reproach in her voice, even though the hubbub has been going on for hours, doorbell ringing, fresh faces coming into the light, lit by it, others retreating to the shadows of the garden, standing in the cool night air. So soon? she will say, accepting an anonymous kiss, more bottles, flowers, buoyed up by it, the eddying motion round her, voices toing and froing, words rising and breaking, a touch on the shoulder, a glance lit by amusement, and all of them here, in her room now, the otherwise empty room, filling it up with sound, with words being uttered, with recognised features, with memorised names.

Discourteous perhaps, but unkind to hint at an ending, this night dying, so I tell myself. As her head turns, I slip out of the room.

2

Cool night air, wind in the trees. Leaf shadows stirring in lamplight. I breathe deeply, see the shadow of a cat streak across the empty road. Opening up between rooftops, trees, a high dark sky with its thin scattering of stars. I too am opening up now, hearing my footfalls in the silent street, breathing, looking up into the high abyss, cool midnight. I need this, not knowing why. To hear my own heart beat, feel my breathing, the slow sad music of night, of soul. I feel myself opening up, a ghostly moonflower, folding back petals to the night, its fragrance set free by the dark. My head is empty, listening for whatever comes into it.

Where did you get to? I've been looking everywhere for you.

He is out of breath from running.

I'm sorry?

I went off to get a drink, and when I came back you'd vanished.

Had I? I'm sorry. I didn't really think you meant to

come back. I thought you were just making an excuse to get away.

I'm sorry. What kind of shit did you take me for?

I didn't. Just your average male.

Oh.

Don't look so hurt. You know what it's like at parties. You get stuck in a corner with someone you find utterly boring, and in the end, if nobody else comes along to join in, you simply have to find a pretext to break it up. I must just speak to so-and-so, for example. But you'd already told me you didn't know a soul. That left: I must find a drink.

You take a very cynical view of human nature.

No, I don't. Besides, finding an excuse to escape lets the other one off the hook too.

Oh. So you were glad to see the back of me.

I didn't say that. What I meant is, sometimes when you are stuck with just one other person, you know perfectly well that they would rather move off, and that they feel trapped too, so you are doing the right thing anyhow. It's a sort of etiquette, really. A bit like dancing the minuet in the old days. Only nowadays we have to learn the steps as we go along. Listening, not to the music, but to the sub-text.

The what?

The sub-text. To what is really going on, what people are really saying.

This is too deep for me. So what did you think I was actually saying, when I said I needed a drink?

Do you really want to know?

Yes.

Now I'm embarrassed.

Tough. You were the one who obviously misread this sub-text of yours.

Well, I thought you probably found me a bit boring, too earnest, intellectual, whatever. Not much fun. And I thought you had probably caught sight of some blonde bimbo on the other side of the room, who took your fancy. Or, if not, that you were hoping to find such a girl on your way to the drinks.

I think you've got a very low opinion of men.

Maybe.

Or of yourself.

No, I don't think so. I'm quite proud, really. That's why I didn't wait to be stood up by you.

You could call it a self-defence mechanism. Rejecting someone before they reject you. Some people would call it a classic symptom of low self-esteem.

Oh would they. Is that what you call it?

No. But I don't talk about sub-texts either.

Touché. By the way, I'm Anna.

And I'm Daniel.

Hi, Daniel.

I proffer my hand in mock formality. We both laugh.

Do you live near here?

Just round the corner. I'd ask you in, but –

Why don't we go to the Café Bleu for coffee? It's not far.

All right, I say brightly, not arguing now, though it will mean a long walk back to my digs.

And so we sit, not arguing now, occupying a small table, confronting but not arguing, no, simply confiding, artlessly, artfully perhaps, randomly, but not, things which spill out of us, out of memory, thought, emotion, drawn out as if from a childish box of found things, kept forever, to be shown now, in this intimate corner, the beginnings of knowing, of showing: this, and this, and this. I think, I was, I remember. Holding this prism, feather, ocean-swept stone. Touching, fondling, holding it up, turning it round. I see it reflected in his dark eyes, he looks for it in mine.

I do not know how long we sit. But the night is just beginning, growing young. I do not know how long we sit, but the room is empty now except for us. When he was five he had an accident with the bread knife: I see the thin scar which grew with him. I think, he says, my fascination with blood started there. But the decision to do medicine was made for him, it runs in the family. As a child they always went to the Alps, winter and summer. He is the result of a skiing romance. Are they happy, I ask, are they happy? I think so, he says. My mother has what she wants, my father also. Grumbling is part of the pact.

I think, I say, I have been fearful always, since birth. And did not know it. Does that make sense? I watch my mother, and feel bad. I feel bad about going, especially this last term. I want to go, that is the worst of it. I can't wait to get out at the beginning of term. When I sat on the platform at King's Cross I was singing out loud. I couldn't help it, really. It sounds irrational, doesn't it, but I can't forgive either of them, not for what they are doing to each other, but for spoiling my childhood. In retrospect. I want everything to be as I thought it was then, preserved in amber for ever.

Perhaps it really was like that then. Things change. Anyhow, what you remember is the truth. What do you remember?

I remember lying under a tree in the garden and thinking that the wind and the leaves speak a different language, and I would give anything to know what they were saying. And you?

I remember climbing the tree in our garden and getting stuck in it for what seemed like hours. It was a very hot day, and I could see the girl next door sunbathing topless, which was a bit of a thrill, but getting down was a real problem. I didn't dare call for help, because I knew perfectly well I wasn't supposed to be up there anyhow – I'd been told off before for ripping a shirt or something. So I sat up there, hoping nobody would see me, especially the girl oiling her boobs. Every time I looked down, trying to get a foothold, the problem just seemed to get worse. I suffer from vertigo now – I think that's how it started. Serves me right, I suppose.

So what did you do in the end?

What could I do? I thought about staying up there for ever, eating leaves. I watched the sun going down, the shadows lengthen on the lawn, and finally I sort of let myself drop. I got off with a badly sprained ankle and a bit of bruising. I think I must have told a few lies about how it happened. My mother usually pretended to believe me. Or rather, she'd give me a funny look, so I knew she knew, but say nothing. I guess she was pretty shrewd. But at that age you think your parents know everything. That they can read your thoughts, see through solid walls, anything.

Big Mother is watching you. I know. Trying to keep things secret at any cost. When I started keeping a diary I went to incredible lengths to make sure she never found it. Truly obvious places like my underwear drawer.

And did she find it?

No idea. To be honest, I think she was more interested in finding out if I had gone on the pill without her permission, that sort of thing.

My worst moment was when she found some girlie magazines in my room. I must have been all of twelve at the time. She was looking for dirty socks, that's all, because I hadn't put any in the laundry basket. I was so ashamed, I can't tell you – I kept saying that a boy at school had made me buy them, that I didn't really want to, throw them away, on and on. I just went on talking so she couldn't get a word in.

And what happened?

She couldn't stop laughing, actually.

It's awful when parents do that. I hated my father for a week after he made fun of a poem I had written about the superior wisdom of dolphins. I remember ocean rhymed with notion. Nevertheless, he was treading on my dreams, and not doing it kindly.

Is this your dream?

What? Riding a dolphin?

No. Writing poetry. You keep on about writing.

It was. It is. I don't know. It's so hard. I know now, you see, that you can't rhyme ocean with notion. I'm getting an education, I know that much now. When

I've been up here for three years I shall know everything, what not to do, how not to do it, who said what when, and how, and how many times, till the words died on him, or her, so all you can do is echo, echo. I don't know. Who am I, after all?

You are you. A unique collection of genes coming together at a particular moment in time, which has never been before, and will never be again.

Yes, but using a common language. That's the problem, you see. It's like passing a coin around day by day. It gets worn down, loses definition, its hard edges. And half the time people don't even notice, they're so busy shopping, putting it in slot machines, whatever.

I don't follow. After all, the coin doesn't lose it's value. You can still buy a loaf of bread with it. The slot machine won't spit it out.

That's just the point, don't you see? I'm not putting this very well. Good poetry doesn't come out of a slot machine. If all you want is a loaf of bread, fine, but man does not live by bread alone.

That did come out of a slot machine!

Sorry, but you know what I mean.

Yes, I do know what you mean. So just what is the problem?

I don't know. If I knew, perhaps we wouldn't be having this conversation. I'd know the answer. It's not a question of finding different words, at least, I don't think so. More a question of making them feel different, so people take notice.

Is that so difficult?

I think so.

Making it new, as they say.

Precisely.

But it is new, anyway, for you. Find your own words for it, whatever it is.

I'll try. But I'm not even sure I've got anything to say.

Perhaps that's the problem.

Perhaps.

3

Good morning. Yes, it is a good morning, but why? The time is coming up to seven forty-nine. Traffic is heavy on the M11 between junctions seven and nine. An accident has closed the Blackwell Tunnel. I draw back the curtains: dazzling sunlight enters. Silvery, not gold. Good morning. A fine dry start to the day, cloud later, the possibility of an occasional shower, a band of rain coming in from the west overnight. Further outlook unsettled. But this is a good morning, I do not know why. Two hundred people feared dead in China, air disaster. Too far off to count, as nobody I know is, or was, bound for Peking. Tough, but I feel good, with silvery light running in, sharp, this glinting sword. When I have drunk my first cup of black coffee, begun to pick up the threads of my life, I will find out why. Another shooting, the usual, so far nobody claiming responsibility, or if, I did not hear, but the secretary of state is saying the usual.

Outrage. Cowardly act. Whoever it was not will do it tomorrow. Must buy bread. Linguistic Theory at eleven. What did I do with my notes?

I am singing. Why? Oh what a beautiful morning. Not a cloud in the sky, nothing. If I could only remember where I put my notes. I've got a beautiful feeling, everything's going my way. Apart from my ruddy notes. And my essay should have been in yesterday. Think up something later. Dow Jones, Hong Kong, interest rates expected to rise. Which reminds me, must ask Dad for a cheque to see me through. It will mean listening to him for half an hour, but I don't see how else, really I don't. He'll cough up, I know. I'll offer to pay him back, the way I did last time. As for my essay, I'll think up some excuse, anything as long as it's not the party. The party! Last night, the party, of course. Talking afterwards with him. What was it that was so unusual, special, head-turning? Perhaps I was a bit drunk. No, I remember clarity, a clear night sky, words forming on a thought, growing, rising luminous, numinous, growing strong as they took off into the night sky, heading for the unknown. I must have been drunk. Probably so much hot air if I heard it now, levitating precariously on wine fumes, swinging wildly on the night wind, on a trip to nowhere. I must have let myself go, hope I did not make a complete ass of myself. Such a relief after that dreadful party, that was it, letting go, releasing the balloon at long last, talking into the night.

The lecturer is late. We sit, sunshine slanting

through the high windows, waiting for him. A buzz of conversation, indistinct. I hear traffic beyond the windows, the world going about its material business, delivering bread and such. I must buy bread. Alice is sitting below me. She turns round, waves, smiles, gestures that she will see me afterwards, outside. I nod, vigorously, showing that I have understood her mouthing, finger pointing. I feel good, I would rather sit by the river with a book, not reading, watching the clouds drift by in a green daydream. I look at my notes, which seem remarkably sparse, considering. A few disjunctive propositions, cut loose from whatever led to them, or followed after. I do not know why I put them down, not now. Often my pen cannot keep up with what is being said, and I give up on the notion, whatever it might have been. Bits of it now floating free, meaningless. I am hopelessly adrift, I know it. What I have understood so far will not get me through, not in a million years. Just bits, here and there, sudden insights, without coherence.

The conversational hum dies suddenly: the speaker has belatedly arrived. Stepping on to the podium, he spreads out his papers, looks up. He begins with a joke, ingratiating but also sarcastic, smiling drily. With his bony cranium, flicking the wings of his gown, he looks like a huge black crow settling. His delivery is staccato, beak going up and down, showing off big juicy worms to his audience, slowing down his rather hurried delivery when displaying the fattest titbits to us. Wittgenstein suddenly pops into view, wriggling ludicrously as the predatory beak pulls him out of the ground. Laughter, another joke coming up. We are privileged to share in the complicity of mocking, this is a titbit he throws us. Unexpectedly, Plato is dragged up from the underworld, but turns out to be only his shadow. This crow, I think, is hopping about with impunity, a scavenger with carefully preened feathers. He picks up shiny things, flashing them ostentatiously, only to discard them a moment later. Rubbish, old bottle tops, mirror shards left behind by previous tenants. Finds a few dry crumbs left over from a historic picnic. Nothing continuous, no continuity to hold us. A beady eye for the crack, the gap in the hedge, fissure, or nest left unattended. Old feathers found in a ditch.

The sloping sunbeam is thick with dust. I hear the world turning beyond the window, concrete, blissfully ignoring all of this, spinning busily on its axis. I think I should not be here either. I am not taking this in, not really. Only half my mind is on it. The other half is mocking this old crow prancing on his podium, showing off, this jackdaw picking through a gigantic rubbish tip. I did not come here for this. I do not know why, but I find it absurd. Having nothing to do with living, breathing, asking the baker for bread. Even less with vision, insight, or finding wings. This has to do with graduating *cum laude*, speaking a language which can only be understood by the few, a privileged discourse. Excluding butcher and baker and candlestick maker. Gown versus town. I am suddenly conscious of echoes, reverberations. How many dust motes can dance in a beam of light? Men

99

thinking in a dead language. He stands, this professor, where he has stood for centuries, attempting to comprehend the universe, trying to pin it down with words fashioned for doing it, qualifying, arguing, turning evil into good, common sense into uncommon nonsense, justifying that which leaves us numb and speechless, trying to make us submit.

You have to give him credit for it. Even though I want to take flight, into the upper air. Even though I know words should have wings, lift us, carry us off. Turning us into white birds on the foam of the sea. How they can do this, why they must, for us to be fully born, this is what I want to know. But, watching the dust motes thick in the falling sunlight, hearing the words strung together with such tenacious industry, I feel I ought to try and follow, give him his due. This is the human race doing its thing, and I am part of it. I could have chosen another terminology, but I chose this. This is man doing his thing, spinning a theoretical web across the void so blindly, urgently, ready to start afresh if the wind blows, or a new broom strikes unexpectedly. 'Tis all in peeces, all cohaerence gone. Words I was using in the essay I have not got to grips with yet. A patterning instinct in us, a need maybe. I must start it again, rethink. Not merely imagery, not just novelty, but trying to fit it all in. Man hath weav'd out a net, not just of meridians and parallels to catch the stars, but the whole caboodle, the works. Trying so hard to catch the fly, even if he turns out to be the fly, stuck in his own thought.

I would rather be a fly, winging out through the

open window, ignoring all this. But perhaps I cannot do without it, must apply myself. Quantifying, qualifying, connecting, putting the fly in the fly-bottle, watching him beat his inexpressible colour into the hard structure to see how he ticks. But the fly does not need to know how, or why. The moment I take off the lid he will go for the open window.

Did you understand any of that?

Alice finds me in the busy corridor.

I think so. Bits of it, anyhow.

It is wonderful to be walking into the open air, to smell grass, a hidden flowering in the wind, to feel gravel crunching firmly with every step. I pull back my shoulders, walk upright.

But I can't help feeling he's wrong. Or rather, it is.

Oh?

Alice is impressed, I can hear as much in her tone.

It's not as simple as that. Or rather, it's not as difficult. Do you see what I'm getting at?

Well, it's got to be one or the other, surely. Or am I being more than usually stupid this morning?

We are standing at the kerb, waiting to cross. Alice yawns exaggeratedly.

Great party, by the way.

It was, wasn't it? Even if I do say so myself.

What I mean is –

But my words are rendered inaudible by a heavy lorry and when we get to the other side of the street Alice is only interested in finding a table. The café is full, and she has not had any breakfast. We find an empty table behind the coat stand.

I'm dying for coffee.

A baby starts doing it quite naturally.

Doing what? Try and catch her eye. I've got a tutorial at noon.

Trying to talk.

So?

So perhaps it's just something we do, as a species, like using two feet for walking.

So what are we doing here? Why am I busting my brains week after week, trying to get a grip on the groundwork?

Good question. Because that's part of being human too. Theorising, asking questions.

I know somebody else who has been asking questions.

What are you talking about?

Come on, don't act the innocent with me.

In the ensuing silence, Alice looks arch over the rim of her coffee cup.

This Daniel person, she says finally. He rang me this morning.

Oh?

I didn't even know who he was, for God's sake. I didn't invite him.

Somebody called Adrian somebody or other brought him.

So I gather. He got my number from Adrian.

So? Why did he ring?

Ah. Wouldn't you like to know.

You brought it up, Alice. I didn't. It's really nothing to do with me.

It has everything to do with you, and you know it.

Come on, spill the beans.

I know no such thing, and there aren't any beans to spill. You're the one who is being all mysterious.

Well, he rang at the crack of dawn, at least it seemed like that to me, but then I didn't get to bed till nearly three. And of course I didn't have a clue who he was. Anyhow, he was very apologetic, about everything really, coming to the party and not talking to me, about ringing up now, so early, but he thought he might have left something behind, an address book, or a filofax or something. Anyhow, I could tell it was just a pretext.

What for?

What do you think? Well, at first I thought he might have taken a fancy to me without my knowing anything about it. People do sometimes, you know. When I was fifteen a boy used to follow me home from school every day, and I only found out about it when his sister told me after it had been going on for a year.

I thought you had a tutorial at noon.

And then I found out he wanted to know about you.

What sort of things?

Mainly, whether you had anybody. A fella.

And what did you tell him.

I said no. That you were a dyke.

You didn't!

No, of course not. Don't worry. I said you had lots of admirers, naturally, looking the way you do, but that you were far too intelligent to fall for just anybody.

Alice, you're a treasure.

I know I am. And for that you can buy my coffee. I've got to rush.

4

I sit at the window with a blank sheet of paper in front of me. I should be writing, but I am staring out through the glass. I see trees in their full summer glory, and sky. In the sky I see clouds. C-L-O-U-D. I listen to the word as though for the first time. It is very odd: suddenly a perfectly ordinary word will sound utterly alien, as though it were foreign, heard for the first time. As if it were a pebble rolling about in my mouth, with my tongue testing its oddity, feeling its strange contours, round, bulging. It is a clod with breath blown into it, my lips send the thing skyward by breathing out vowels, exhaling them into its solidity and puffing it upward. But I sit down here and it flies high in the sky, immensely far off. I call it cloud, this clod of water vapour, and think nothing of it, day in, day out. But now, suddenly, I am overcome by its strangeness, my mind is taken aback by its own function. The connection between sound and thing is missing, arbitrary, absurd.

I sit at the window, doing nothing. Struck by the absurdity of my mouth forming the word cloud, which I hear for the first time. Watching the thing in the sky, just as odd.

I must shut out the trees, their branches thick with leaf. I must shut out the odd thing suspended overhead, slowly moving. I begin to write, consulting my notes, looking up a quotation. The words begin to flow. But I suddenly find myself hesitating: 'if' has only two letters to it, and looks very peculiar. I do not know why, but it looks as though something is missing. I know I have not misspelt it, but it looks as if I had. Standing by itself, it looks barbarous, raw, a crude monosyllable reaching back to pre-history. It looks to me like a branch of wood with something lopped off it.

5

Two cups between us, both of us leaning forward. But neither of us is saying much. Odd. The other night we could hardly stop. A veil of shyness now. Whilst waiting for our coffee he asked me about work, and I told him I was writing an essay on John Donne, but finding it difficult. I was hoping he would respond with an outburst of enthusiasm, so I could share it with him, finding this in common. But he just looked thoughtful, saying nothing, and now I feel awkward about launching into a eulogy without being given my cue. So instead I ask him about his work, and he begins telling me at some length but, noticing, no doubt from the expression on my face, that his terminology is beyond me, offers a diffident apology for boring me.

No, no, I say. Teach me. I want to learn.

Some other time, he says. It's really not that interesting. Just part of the process.

So now we sit with two full cups between us, saying nothing. Both of us leaning with forearms on the marble top, heads almost touching, gazing down into our coffee. I toy with my spoon, touching the froth.

The table is next to the window. The sky, grey all morning, is darkening further. Now the first drops of water splatter the pane, streak down. He looks up from stirring his coffee, we both look out, at this grey world, the blurring vision of figures hurrying. As long as we stay here, lingering over our coffee, we are dry, safe. We are both smiling, catching each other's eye.

England, he says.

Yes, I say.

If the Eskimos really do have four hundred words for snow, we should have as many for rain.

We've got quite a few.

Shower.

Downpour.

Drizzle.

Mizzle.

Cats and dogs.

We both laugh. The window is fogging up. I write my name, ANNA, in the steam.

I used to do that as a child, I say. I still can't resist doing it.

Must have been the first word you learnt to write.

Yes, I used to get the Ns back to front.

That's how they'll see it outside, if anybody looks in. As it's the same back to front.

A palindrome.

A what?

A palindrome. You know – Able was I ere I saw Elba.

What has Napoleon to do with it? Oh, I get it. Very ingenious. Got any more like that tucked away?

Afraid not. You'd have to ask my kid brother, Harry. He could probably tell you a few. He used to love that kind of stuff when he was younger. Awful puns, silly riddles.

I've only got a sister, and she's older than me. Rather serious really. Going to be a GP.

So it runs in the family – medicine, I mean?

I'm afraid so. Father, and an aunt. Not very original, is it? Doing what my father did. Does.

Oh, I don't know. I think it's rather nice. At least you've got a sense of continuity, of really being a family. Not like mine.

A pause. I turn my head and look at the window, where the word ANNA has begun to run down the pane, rivulets of tears coursing relentlessly down, spoiling things. Spoiling everything. I try blinking, biting my lip. I do not know how to go on. Anna through the looking glass, shrinking now.

I rub out my running name from the glass. It has stopped raining.

It's stopped raining, I say.

Yes, he says.

They're divorcing, I say. My parents.

I'm sorry.

I spoon the froth from out of my cup, into my mouth. Look at the people entering, leaving. I do not look at him.

Well, I say, and shrug. I turn to look at him. I thought I was grown up, I say.

You look pretty grown up to me.

So why do I feel this resentful? So hurt and angry?

Because you're still Anna, he says. You're still the same person. Just because you've got bigger doesn't mean you're somebody else, any more than Alice was when she drank the potion.

I stare at him. That's odd.

What is?

You saying that.

My saying what?

About Alice. That's just what I was thinking. About her getting bigger and then shrinking.

Still in her little girl clothes.

Yes, I say.

Curiouser and curiouser, he says.

Yes.

We both laugh.

6

Stillness, night, no words. I need to feel this, utterance falling away. No words. I need to sit here, singular, under this dark translucent heaven, the earth beneath. I need to hear it, this stillness, the breath of it, the breathing quietly, holding earth to water to sky. I need to breathe with it, inhaling the breath of it, stirring through trees now, touching my skin. I hear a fish plop, a branch creak, the shadow of a weeping willow sigh. Tiny sounds defining the immensity of it, growing in the night. Sitting, dumb. Swimming in it, washing off everything, liquid night sky rippling through my fingers, moon, stars, everything. No thought, no nothing. Feeling grass under my skin, hearing a night bird, looking at shadows, light glimmer, the far-off sky. In it, of it, perceiving. Nothing coming between us, constructs, famous lines, history. Just wind on my skin, sky rippling on water, cradling a broken moon in its flow. This is it, nothing but this.

7

I feel as though I am treading on eggshells, rather self-conscious. We are both self-conscious, I in my high heels and low neckline, he in his dinner jacket. He has bought the most expensive tickets in the hall: I can tell from where we have been sitting. Before going into the auditorium he bought, unnecessarily, two programmes, and handed me one. Moving out now, I hear the crisp rustle of silk with my every step. Treading warily, I am conscious of spaces, handrails, mirroring surfaces. I have been to the hairdresser. I think Daniel has too: something neat about his ears.

I feel I should say something about the music we have been listening to, but nothing much occurs to me, and Daniel is so terrifyingly knowledgeable. His mother plays the piano and his father is a keen amateur cellist. They play duets. Daniel learnt the flute – he hastens to say he is not terribly good – and joins in for trios. I feel shut out, inept. I was unfamiliar with the pieces played in the first half, and trying to get my mind round the programme notes did not help much. When I got to the end of a paragraph I had already forgotten the beginning. I was being dutiful, going through the motions. Daniel had paid too much for the thing. Three movements, I remembered, and E flat. Clueless about keys, at least I would know when it was over, and not make a fool of myself by clapping too soon.

We stand, holding our drinks, watching the people come and go, speaking casually of this and that, not, I should think, Michelangelo, but possibly, dauntingly, of pitch, contrapuntal composition, variations of tempo, expressive licence. I say, timidly, that I thought the soloist was very good, and Daniel agrees. It is, he says, a difficult piece. My eye is caught by a tall man with grey hair on the far side of the bar, talking animatedly. His features are vaguely familiar, and I think he must be famous, perhaps a critic or a programme organiser. I am suddenly conscious of my youth: inexperienced, gauche, despite the sleek hairdo and the rustling silk, gawping at concert-goers who no doubt do this sort of thing every night of the week. I think Daniel and I are play-acting, dressing up, going through the motions of an old-fashioned dance in unfamiliar finery. I feel shy, struck by his good looks, cleanshaven, smooth.

The best is yet to come, says Daniel, referring to the second half of the programme, a Mahler symphony.

I love Mahler, I say, listening to the stupid inadequacy of my own words. I cannot think of anything to add.

Schubert too, says Daniel, and I feel better, since he is not getting any further.

I pretend to sip from my glass, which is almost empty. I would feel foolish, holding an empty glass, and I see nowhere to put it nearby. Nor do I want Daniel to see me holding an empty glass. I would then have to protest that, no, I do not want another drink. I look longingly, with unashamed curiosity, as people stand, singly or in groups, men with women, talking, drinking, strolling to look out through the window at the grey river. A woman with dyed red hair in a short black dress, wearing heavy jewellery. An old man too frail to stand unaided, leaning precariously on his stick, spine bent and head pushed forward, to see, listen, hear. A young girl is holding his elbow, bending to catch his words. What do they know, these others, how do they think? Could they tell me something I know nothing of? I feel an unspoken secret. It is this which brings the old man who can hardly stand, the young girl who helps him sit down.

We hear the melodious signal for the second half of the concert sounding through the building. A soft repetition in, says Daniel, the tuning key of A. I measure my steps to its beat as we walk, *andante moderato*, towards the double doors of the auditorium. There is a slight hold-up here, the concert-goers awkwardly clustering round the entry, but studiously ignoring this propinquity, trying not to touch, eye not meeting eye or, if a glance is accidentally exchanged, the look blank and stony. We are separate, says our body language, and we do not know you. We try to keep a civilised distance at all times, only exchanging words and the eye-light of recognition with those few we already know. Necessity might, for a brief moment, bring us to this, thigh lightly brushing up against thigh, an unexpected inhalation of odour, the sight of an ear with hair in it or dandruff on a dark collar, such proximity will not undermine the sense of being separate which holds us, this poise which naming has given us, huddling together though we are for this moment with the anonymous, no names having been exchanged.

Remarks overheard are also fitting, words being clothing of a sort. Nothing too loud, brash, nothing indecent or nakedly revealing. Ostentation, if at all, must be casual and discreet, like good jewellery, no obvious showing off, just a throwaway remark, jokingly spoken. I, you, each of us clad in unseen armour. Fanning out now, through the spacious auditorium, finding our allotted seats by alphabet and number, tidily spaced, row upon row.

Until the music begins. Suddenly a flood, a great wave breaking, carrying us forward willynilly, tossing us in a hurlyburly of sound. No I now, no you, nothing but a vast ocean in which we are floundering, thrown off balance, perhaps lost. But not lost, no, hearing it, feeling it for the first time, since when, birth perhaps, feeling the armour dissolve, turn to nothingness, sensing the I that was only I swelling, growing, no frontier now, only a language that speaks from beyond words, out of the reach of reason, but reaching far further than either ever could. A language that, if it can be called such, comes from beyond birth, division, heard long ago and since forgotten, its beat now echoing in us, finding its echo, responding after being numb, dumb for so long.

8

We go into the night together. Wordless. It weighs heavily on us, this lack of speech, but forms a bond more eloquent than any utterance. Saying something now could break it, not simply for now but forever. I do not know how I know this, why I feel this certainty, but I have never felt so sure of anything. I think we have both been taken possession of, hearing that which we have just heard, its message tranfiguring us both. That which was to and fro, spoken or withheld, just a playful shuttlecock, flying, artful, neither of us want this now, too trivial, it could only shatter that which is holding us spellbound. I hold it, as I sense he is holding it too, this depth of sound, singing, this thrill which is yearning, bringing its own fulfilment, this ache finding no echo except in sound, phrasing, the rising and sinking, or solo losing out to the immensity, the sound wave breaking.

We walk through the night, hearing our footfalls. Night has transfigured the city too, turning it into a magic network of light, luminous buildings floating on the river, rippling black and silver with light. We stand on the bridge, leaning forward, holding hands. Earth has not anything to show more fair. Everything built is now ethereal, a vision held between earth and sky, nothing sordid, grimy. An eternal city, held by the old river. Sweet Thames run softly till I end my song, for I sing not loud nor long. But now I stand over the tenuous city, hearing dark water lapping. My own breath. I hear the night, the river running, our music flowing through us to the dark, moonlit sea.

9

It is ringing. At last, the telephone is ringing.

Hello.

Hi.

Neither of us speak, a weighty pause. Then:

How are you?

Fine. And you?

Fine too.

Another silence. Then he adds: As a matter of fact, I feel great.

I do too.

You do? I'm glad to hear it.

We listen to each other breathing in the ensuing silence.

I could do with a bit of sleep.

So could I.

Both of us giggling now, slightly.

What are you doing?

Nothing much. I've just washed my hair, and I think I'll have a bath soon.

Mmm. I wish I was there.

I do too.

I could get in the bath with you.

You couldn't. It's not big enough.

Even better.

I hear his laugh, his breathing in my ear. I hold the plastic receiver to my ear, leaning forward in my bathrobe in what is almost a foetal position, knees to chin, cosily. Listening.

Well, he says, I suppose I had better go.

I say nothing, hanging on.

Anna?

Yes.

Are you still there?

Yes.

Are you all right?

I'm fine.

Good. I'll call you tomorrow.

Fine.

Are you sure you're all right?

Of course I am.

Sleep well.

I will. You too.

Goodnight then.
Goodnight.
You hang up first.
No, you.

10

'What the names in language signify must be inde-
structible; for it must be possible to describe the state
of affairs in which everything destructible is destroyed.'

I look at the quotation, but I feel sick. My mind
will not focus, though I try. I know nothing, only
this. I must follow this logic, discuss it, put it in
context. It goes on:

'And this description will contain words; and what
corresponds to these cannot be destroyed, for otherwise the words would have no meaning.'

This is it, giving the words priority, a free-floating
validity superior to mere things. I think. I do not
know whether this is the meaning. If it is, he might be
wrong. Words can be used vaguely, carelessly,
lyingly. Perhaps not intentionally mendacious, but.
Without prior thought, as a result of which everything destructible is destroyed, horribly.

He puts too much trust in the words, I think this is
his flaw. But when everything hangs on it. Tomorrow. He did say tomorrow. I am making too much of
this, perhaps. But I am looking into an abyss, where

everything destructible is destroyed, or was merely an illusion. And if it is an illusion, whatever has been put into words, what of the words then? The confusion grows. I think, re-reading the paragraph, his concept is of mirrors, word and thing tossing to and fro, self-reflexive as an old-fashioned syllogism.

I was a fool, taking words on trust too. In the beginning was the word, coin of the realm of truth. I just heard what I wanted to hear, investing everything. And now tomorrow is dying, dwindling awfully into night. And if tomorrow is tomorrow too, should I think that all is not lost? Better to stop hoping now, do yourself a favour. I could go to the cinema with Alice after all, say I changed my mind. Too bad if he rings tomorrow and I am out. I cannot reach him and, if I could, I would not try. No. Do try to concentrate on the work in hand. 'I must not saw off the branch on which I am sitting.' *Ich darf mir nicht den Ast absägen, auf welchem ich sitze.* Am I about to do this, too proud, too hasty, jumping to conclusions? Perhaps. No point in cutting off my nose to spite my face, *mir die Nase absägen.* Tomorrow would still do, but pretend not to mind, whatever else you do, play it cool. Perhaps, after all, we do not speak the same language, and his sense of tomorrow is rather less urgent, infinitely more flexible, according to what comes up. Translating to soon, this week, some time in the not too distant future. *Man lernt das Spiel, indem man zusieht, wie Andere es spielen.* One learns the game by watching how others play, acting, adjusting accordingly.

The telephone begins to ring. Ringing, ringing. But it is not him. My mother's voice sounds plaintive.

Anna?

I feel fury rising, my pulse slowing miserably. I do not wish her to interrupt my thoughts, intruding now.

How are you?

Fine.

I sound terse, on purpose. Nor do I wish to hear what she has to say, which is bound to be unpleasant, one way or another.

Are you all right?

My entire universe is in turmoil, I think my heart is breaking even as I speak.

Of course I'm all right. Why shouldn't I be?

Only you sound so snappy.

It's just that I'm working. Wittgenstein.

Who?

You know, Wittgenstein, the philosopher.

I didn't know you were doing philosophy.

I'm not. It's just that – oh, it's too hard to explain.

Try me. I'm not a complete idiot.

I never said you were. It's just that I'm doing linguistic theory as an option.

I see. Sounds interesting.

It's bloody difficult, actually. I'm beginning to think it was a bad idea.

You'll manage.

Perhaps. How did you get on at the hospital?

All right. I'm in the clear, apparently.

That's good news.

Yes, it is.

Any other news?

No. Oh yes. Your father is going to marry that girl.

This is the punch-line, everything has been leading up to this. I sit down suddenly, winded.

No.

Oh yes. Your father more or less said so.

Your father, your mother, this possessive pronoun flying to and fro for months, accusingly, their barbed arrows, I as pig in the middle shrieking with agonised fury. A plague on both your houses. I want to hear nothing, not from either of them.

When?

Last night.

Are you sure? Perhaps he's just trying to wind you up.

No, I think he means it. Anyway, why should it bother me? If he wants to make a fool of himself, that's his problem. I just thought you should know.

Thanks.

I know you don't like her.

I never said that. I hardly know her.

So you wouldn't mind?

Of course I mind. I mind about everything – selling the house, you two going on at each other, everything.

It's hardly my fault.

I never said it was. It's just the way you bring it up. Your father, you say, as though I was responsible for him. And he's as bad.

Why? What does he say about me?

Nothing. Not usually. Except that when he does have to refer to you he does the same thing – your mother, he says, tell your mother, speak to your mother about it. I'm sick of it.

I'm sorry. I'll try to keep things to myself in future, if that's how you feel. It's not exactly been easy for me you know, this past year or two.

I know that.

I never wanted this, ever. You've got your whole life in front of you, but I –

Mum –

I thought you were old enough to understand, that I could rely on you for a bit of support.

He's still my father.

I know. It's hard on you. I shouldn't vent my anger on you.

That's okay.

No, it's not. I open my stupid mouth without thinking. I should count to ten, as my father used to say.

Really?

It was one of his maxims, when we were children. That you can't unsay words, once they're out, so it's best to take a deep breath and count to ten, if in doubt.

Did it work?

Up to a point. We knew better than to argue with him, or challenge his authority. Will you be coming down soon?

I don't know. I don't think so. It depends.

On what?

Oh, things.

Does he have a name?

Mother!

Well, does he?

Yes, as a matter of fact. It's Daniel.

Daniel. So bring him down.

I don't know. I don't know anything at the moment.

Like that, is it?

Sort of.

My poor darling. I expect it'll sort itself out. You want to tell your old mum about it?

No.

Okay. Call me.

II

We could, he says, stay in. I hear him saying 'we' and concur. I will not go out into the cold, the empty night. Not necessary now: this I, solitary perpendicular, struggling to stay upright, passing through this door, the next. When we return, shutting the door, pushing the bolt firmly, he holds my icy fingers between his hands, warming them up. Two halves have become one whole, lying snugly within their skin. We will light a fire and sit by it, reflecting its glow. If the night wind blows through the hollow roof I will turn and find him, the half into which I fit. I have forgotten much: old clothing, the perilous path into the unknown, even the syllables of the name to which I was born. We sit, we speak, we touch.

We speak by touching, mingling our two halves. I

divulge secrets I did not know of, as that which was I melts into him, us. Our fingertips reading our skin blindly, sending messages by touch, lightly, instantly, without interpreter. Each question its own answer in this interchange, the dumb tongue searching in the dark, probing for response. Which, when it comes, is violent, its cry barbaric.

We let go, drifting idly, cast off from our moorings. Nothing can harm us now. I plus I is this, this protective flesh, smelling sweet as a peach, with us its kernel. I get up, its scent still on me. We both get up. We are planning to go out. Next year, we are planning to go to Italy.

12

Tell me about him.

This is the cue I have been waiting for. Whilst we discussed her journey up, Harry's schooling, Granny's hip replacement, and whether to have fish or chicken. All through lunch, catching up on the family gossip, filling her in on my various activities during the term, I have been dying to speak of it, my metamorphosis, my heart like a singing bird now, this bliss with which I am bursting. Bursting to spill it all. But now, when the moment has come, I am suddenly tongue-tied.

Well, his name is Daniel Wolfson.

My mother sits, waiting. Her face is worn, indelible shadows under her eyes, grey streaks now in her thick hair. Experience sits on her like dust.

Yes?

Everything I say, anything I would wish to say is bound to sound foolish.

He's doing medicine, and I met him at a party. Quite by chance, actually. He'd been brought along by a friend.

I see.

This is my mother, but not. I cannot lay my head in her lap, be held. Nor jump up and down excitedly. I am grown up now, we both act accordingly. Her tired eyes look at me differently, having been through too much.

And . . . he's studying medicine.

Nothing of this is what I really want to say. That I am happy, happy. That I have found him. My heart like a singing bird. Delirium. I cannot say this. I would look foolish, to her.

Is that all you're going to tell me?

A slightly mocking, but fond smile. She knows there is much, much more to tell. I do not trust her sufficiently. The break-up with my father has turned her into a cynic of sorts.

He likes music a lot. All his family play.

We lean back as our ice creams are brought to the table. My mother orders coffee for both of us. Spooning up chilly chocolate and vanilla brings an echo of our old relationship, my childhood. I savour it, scraping up the melting dregs.

Have you met any of his family?

Not yet.

Instead of her wedding ring, my mother now wears a greenish stone heavily set in silver.

That's new, I say.

Yes, she says. I bought it.

She answers almost curtly, defiantly. I respect her for it, for picking herself up, going out to buy a ring as proof. I lower my spoon, look her in the eyes.

His family is Jewish.

So?

So nothing. I'm just telling you, since you asked about him.

13

We sit in a ring of light, shut in by dark, by music. Bach, his double concerto. We sit on the floor, I leaning against an armchair, his back to the worn sofa. My left foot touching his right. Light shed by the lamp shuts us in, with a bottle of wine, two glasses and only a plate between us. I was a boy scout, he says, and puts the last mushroom into my mouth with his fork. This reminds me, sitting in the dark. I don't see you as a boy scout, I say, my words spiralling round his, easily, as the two violins speak to each other, airily interweaving. His mother, he says, found this a solution to unending summer holidays. When I was about twelve I found beach holidays boring.

I always wanted a Wendy house, I say. In the

summer I sat under an old sheet strung up near the apple tree. I could see the light through it, shadows of leaves dancing. I lean forward, put a morsel of bread in my mouth, seeing my own shadow looming on the ceiling. The pattern of sound weaving its spell round us, echoing us, this harmony.

I lift my glass to the light. It glows, ruby-red. Drink up, he says, thrusting the bottle towards me. I sip, the glow running through my body, my head slightly detached, swimming with music. I feel, I say, putting my head back, seeing my shadow on the far ceiling, as though I was weightless, floating. Defying gravity. A balloon bouncing happily on the end of a string. The sound of my own words is pleasing, playful. You hold the string, I think, but say nothing. His hand is lying inert on my ankle, but his look, dark and inward, tells me that he is listening to the music, only the music. Does he hear me through it? I recognise this look from coitus, so near, so far, his head intent on its inner message. I think we hear each other through it, this echo from far off.

Part Four

I

I've never been so terrified in my life, said Jonathan, lifting his wine glass. I was suddenly in this enormous space full of swarthy men wearing weird clothes, like a lot of nightshirts, not a pair of trousers in sight, and I realised that if I did not find my father in this seething mass I was lost, utterly lost.

Everybody is listening to Jonathan now, all eyes on him. This is not just gossip, it is a story, and the focus is on him. It gives me the opportunity to go to the kitchen, drain the vegetables, thicken the gravy. There is a moment in any dinner party when the conversation gathers its own momentum, without further prodding from the host. This is it. I hear laughter from the kitchen, Jonathan's voice in control.

It wasn't just that I didn't know the language. I couldn't even read the signs. It never entered my head that there wouldn't be a sign spelling out EXIT or PASSPORT CONTROL in normal Roman letters. I mean, I'm not a complete duffer, and even Greek or Russian lettering I could possibly have figured out eventually. But in Arabic it's just loops and squiggles, and you can't even tell where one letter ends and the next one begins.

Backwards too, Arabella says brightly.

Arabella did not go with him on this trip, which he took before they met, but she has heard the story frequently, and can add a few grace notes. She is watching him, the others too, gauging their attention span.

It could have been upside down, for all I knew. Talk about culture shock. I mean, I wasn't expecting the last vestiges of empire, but I suppose I have come to regard English as the lingua franca, if you'll pardon the expression, as far as air travel is concerned.

Daniel is going round the table, topping up glasses. Help yourselves, I say, putting down a dish of steaming carrots garnished with butter and parsley. Nobody hears. Godfrey looks uneasy, sitting silently next to Arabella. I must, I think, find a topic which will bring him in soon. If Jonathan stops for breath.

He felt as though he had landed on a different planet, prompts Arabella.

Absolutely. Jonathan is almost shouting now. There was no way I could communicate with these hordes of men milling round in nightshirts –

Galabiyahs, mutters Godfrey, but loud enough to be heard.

What?

They're called galabiyahs.

Jonathan is looking at Godfrey as though he had not seen him until now. Everybody turns to look at him.

You must excuse my husband, Arabella says

sweetly, lightly touching his hand. He has a very odd sense of humour.

Godfrey is blinking rapidly, unsmiling. Not looking directly at anybody round the table. Arabella glances adoringly at her partner, who accepts her teasing barb for what it is, a playful gift. But poor Godfrey has no notion of this lovers' collusion, clearly thinks it was meant for him, implying his failure to pick up on obvious joking, intended irony. And I must admit, though fond of him, he is a bit too solemn for this. No light touch, no letting go. Perhaps it was a mistake to ask him, Daniel had his doubts, but I think he just needs to find the right girl. Putting Ruth on his left is not looking promising, as she has not yet succeeded in finding a way into the conversation either.

You wait, says Arabella loudly, he'll start talking about wogs in a minute, given enough wine. It's the public school coming out in him, lurking under that thin veneer of civilisation.

Darling! What have I done to deserve this? Take no notice of her. She has a very low opinion of my liberal credentials. Thinks I'm really a diehard reactionary at heart.

Jonathan only pretends to sound aggrieved, minds nothing so long as he is the focus of attention. Arabella, vivacious, confident, is his sidekick in this double act. Though her criticism of him is seriously intended, she knows she can utter it now with impunity.

Lovely food, murmurs Ruth, in a momentary hush, whilst the gravy boat passes from hand to hand.

Arabella is distracted by this, Jonathan is chewing a mouthful of food, struck dumb by it. Ruth seizes the opportunity.

To go back to what you were saying earlier, about being in a foreign country. I spent two months in France last year, on my own. And although I thought I really knew French, I soon realised I didn't, not really. I'd get the literal meaning, and then find that in actual fact something completely different was being said. Or just the way it was said, the inflexion, misled me. I wonder whether we can ever really learn a foreign language, the way we learn our own. Which, of course, we never consciously learn at all.

Nobody says anything, for a moment there is a total, embarrassing hush. Referring back to a prior topic is always risky, and Ruth has not helped herself by introducing a new mood with such a tenuous link.

What I can't stand about French, says Arabella, loudly breaking the hush, is the way they say four twenties and a ten every time they want to say ninety. It's so clumsy – you practically need a calculator to know what they're saying.

Now who's being xenophobic? You'll be calling them frogs next.

Not at all. As a matter of fact I regard the French as just about the most civilised nation in the world. It's just that they have this very long-winded way of saying ninety-nine.

But that's just it, you see, Ruth chips in loudly. That's what I mean. I'm sure when a Frenchman says *quatre-vingt-dix-neuf* he thinks of it as one word.

I doubt whether he has to do any mental arithmetic. But English people do. For us it's very odd.

Daniel recalls saying *obrigado* in a Portuguese village, and being met by a flood of words which were utterly incomprehensible to him, after which he felt it was safer not even to try using anything but English. Sheer vanity, he adds, on my part. Studying a phrase book on the flight out.

Suddenly everybody is talking at once. Godfrey tells me about a play he saw last week, urging us to go. Daniel, I sigh, never has time, or he's too tired. Arabella overhears us and the two of them unexpectedly find common cause in discussing the play. Daniel is listening to Ruth, his head perched at an angle, apparently deeply engrossed in what she is telling him. Ruth keeps her voice low, which is probably why Daniel is suddenly so attentive. Ruth needs drawing out. But now Jonathan has caught the gist of their discussion, butted in, and all three are laughing. The rest of the food is cooling. Arabella has just begun to tell me about her new job when Godfrey suddenly remembers he has a message for me, from Clive. Not Clive Masterson? chirps Arabella, and asks whether I have heard that he and Jill are through, no doubt about it, Jonathan thinks Jill too ambitious for any man to put up with, but a little bird has told her that Clive was a bit of a Lothario on the sly, had a tendency to play while the cat was away on one of her foreign trips. I reply that if the little bird was Alice, then I had heard the same story, but that Alice loves to stir things up. Whereupon Arabella retorts not only Alice, looking at me with raised eyebrows, as if challenging me to guess, or tantalise us all with gossip withheld, her mock discretion. I turn to Godfrey, intending to ask for Clive's message, but he has now been drawn into a discussion begun at the far end of the table, on the possibility of developing a world language, and whether this would be a good thing or not.

Daniel thinks it would be awful, drab, just as if all the apples in the world were those tasteless French ones, but Jonathan thinks the global village is with us whether we like it or not. Arabella starts off on the awfulness of French apples whilst Godfrey is trying to assert that cultural imperialism is not a new phenomenon. Think of the Romans, he says, and the world using Latin for centuries. But nobody is listening to him. I wonder whether there really was a message from Clive; if so, I will never hear it now. I go round the table, picking up forgotten plates, gather up the detritus. When I bring in the dessert a chorus of approval greets me, a joyous *tutti*, in harmony.

2

I didn't say that.

Yes you did.

I said I thought it was a pity, that's all.

Meaning what precisely?

Just that. I don't know, I really hadn't given it much thought.

You must have meant something by it. Nobody makes a remark like that out of the blue.

Daniel, what is this — some kind of inquisition?

I just think you're being disingenuous, and I don't like what you're implying.

I wasn't implying anything!

It was pretty obvious to me.

Well then, if it was so bloody obvious, why are you asking me?

Because I want you to admit it, to me and to yourself.

Admit what?

What you really meant.

I keep telling you, I just thought it wouldn't work out. So I said I thought it was a pity. All right?

What makes you think it won't work out?

I don't know. I just feel it in my bones. I really haven't given it much thought.

Which just goes to prove my point.

What point?

You don't like him, and you disapprove of what he is doing.

I never said anything of the sort.

No, but that is what you were implying.

You think.

Yes, I do.

It hardly follows. I mean, if you were right, I wouldn't have said I thought it was a pity.

No?

No. Obviously not. I wouldn't have cared what the outcome was, one way or the other.

Do you mind?

Not that much, no. I'm certainly not going to lose any sleep over it.

So I was right. You don't really like him.

I'm not wild about him, if you really want to know.

At last. Why couldn't you come right out with it?

I don't know. Does it matter?

Of course it does.

I thought you would mind.

I do.

You see.

But that's no reason not to talk about it.

Isn't it?

No. We have to be honest with each other.

Yes, of course.

And that means not holding anything back.

Anything? I'm not so sure. Some things are best left unsaid.

What sort of things?

I can't tell you. That would be telling. Just things.

3

I is now we, us. I know this, I accept it fully. But I feel uneasy, surprisingly so. The discomfort lurks at the back of my mind, niggling. Occasionally it confronts me in the bathroom mirror, on the edges of sleep, when I sit in the dusk listening for his key to turn in the lock. The truth is, I am not, not now. Anna has committed herself to Daniel, and I am out in the cold, a discomforting ghost, tapping beseechingly at windows, trying to speak. I know myself to be out there, looking in, standing in the thickening shadow of the plane tree, hungry, pitifully thin. I keep trying to find an opportunity to let her in, hold her cold hands between mine, rub the warmth back into them, into her, hear what she has to say. I know that she is dying to tell me things, dying from it, the need to tell, that which is for my ears only. But it is too difficult. I find I am about to open the french window, the back door, but get no further. The doorbell rings, or the telephone. I lift the sash of the bedroom window with only moonlight to see by, and he is calling from below. Friends crowd the hours, we have so many between us. His mother will speak, must be spoken to, as well as my own. Now long hours of work, too, occupy us, dividing us from each other, taking up much of the day. Anna through the looking glass after a hasty breakfast looks smart, picks up her briefcase, ready for the day ahead, the conference at eleven, not shy of giving her opinion now, jargon at her fingertips, finding it fun, the gossip, the badinage, this responsibility she will not shirk.

But, she finds herself thinking, suddenly, straphanging in the Underground, shopping for groceries in the late-night store, sitting in the silent hallway with the bags at her feet, the front door shut, coat still round her shoulders, where am I in all this? I cannot hear myself think. I am nothing but a persona, reflecting the world, this busy mirror with its bright facets flashing, out, out.

So, on the nights when Daniel is on duty, when she returns to an empty house, she will stand with her hand on the door for a moment, listening intently to the stillness, the dark spaces rising overhead, its familiar, mysterious breath. And, without turning on lights, tiptoe from room to room, her feet feeling carpet, floorboard, blissfully without shoes on now, stretching, touching, refreshing herself in this dark pool with nobody in it. Only a dim light from the window, and shadows playing on the far wall. I am here now, she whispers. Leaf shadows stirring in an unheard wind. That, and her own breathing. Hearing myself speak, at long last, spirit returning to its body stealthily now, joyously bursting into untrammelled speech for my ears only. So much catching up to do, what I think, feel, know.

4

I am sitting in the square, a pigeon pecking crumbs round my feet. I do not know how much longer I can bring my lunch out here: there is a distinct nip of autumn in the air. As I write, a few leaves are already turning, tumbling earthward. I bring out this notebook with my sandwich, this apple I munch for dessert. The square is a tiny island. My lunch hour is also an island. I sit in it, cutting myself off from everybody, everything.

I do not know why I feel the need to keep this diary, of sorts. Well, yes, I do. How to explain? I do not have a plan. I am not, I think, inching my way forward to a literary endeavour. No. If anything quite the reverse. I have been working, now, long enough to feel distinctly distrustful of such things. The glamour has worn off. I sigh when I see the slush pile, not expecting to find anything. Slush is a good word for it – an amorphous heap of soiled grey paper, lying around too long.

I sit in the square again today. This is my bench now. From this angle I can watch people coming and going, walking the gravel paths, sitting on other benches. This is my hour now, I keep it apart. I avoid my colleagues, slipping away unnoticed. When I am not out for lunch this notebook stays in the bottom drawer of my desk, which locks. It stays there, by itself, at weekends. The bench on which I sit is put here in memory of Miriam Goldsmith. I know nothing of her except that she is not living now. The gravel paths are strewn with fallen leaves, crisp and dry. Everything is tinged with gold. But I must go.

I feel old, suddenly, watching lovers kiss on a nearby bench, hungrily, oblivious. The sky is overcast, dark clouds scudding furiously now. My clothes are not warm enough, a chill wind is blowing, gusting up dry leaves, which whirl and scatter. I think we should have a child, not now perhaps, but soon. It frightens me to think of it, but I do not know what else to do, if life is a progression. Is it? I feel it should be, that there should be a pattern. I am growing old so quickly, with nothing to show for it.

I watch the light changing, moment by moment. Cloud shadows fall across the gravel paths, darken the untidy grass. The sun is bright today, but gives no warmth, coming and going suddenly. I hear traffic thundering by relentlessly. Nothing is still. The black statue in the centre of the square, where all paths meet, stands upright, a human rock of sorts in the whirlpool, slightly ludicrous in his frock-coat, bird droppings discolouring his head and shoulders. Making his pitiful stand against the ever-rolling stream, for now. Nobody noticing much, hurrying by. Busily, busily.

Everything so transient. I put things down, what I see, feel for a moment, which is already over. Writing things down is trying to stop the rot. History begins with it: my own, ours, all story. Remember the worthy in his frock-coat. Do not forget Miriam Goldsmith. This is why I do it, jotting it down, how I sit on a wooden bench whilst an elderly person walks by with her elderly dog, both grey and obese. I feel old, suddenly, seeing the end of summer blowing from the branches nearby. I remember, as a child, thinking about deciduous trees, shuffling through fallen leaves with gusto, looking forward to Christmas, hearing the clock ticking too slowly. Everything evergreen, glowing gold in the firelight. Not now, no. Hold it, just for the moment. Let the last leaf hold to the tree. Let the tree stand, still green, in the cooling sunshine. I, Anna, sit on the bench now, in the moment, seeing this dying, regretting it.

I sit in a sandwich bar, water coursing down the window. Pedestrians hurrying through the downpour. Grey light, grey gutters running fast. Heads hidden under taut umbrellas, held against the wind. I count the shopping days to Christmas without enthusiasm. Daniel, grey with overwork, just wants to sleep. I must think for him, plan a bit. As usual, the window displays are being arranged even earlier than last year, but this might be just my personal impression, everybody's personal impression. Resentment at being coerced into such excessive spending. Perhaps it is not just the shops, but the feeling that each year seems to pass quicker than the last. This job is already a habit, getting in, eyeing the clock without thinking, yesterday's in-tray out. In control, on top of it, but not so thrilling. It was all so exciting at first: I was going to make my mark, find things, bring new thoughts, newly put into words, into the light. I still get that feeling, now and then, seeing a set of fresh proofs sitting on my desk, pristine, snowy white. But not for long, not now. I recall last year's triumph turning to dust, buried in it, forgotten.

Moving on, I should soon do it. Worldly success depends on it. Stand still and you get in a rut, so current wisdom goes. The rut is easy, comforting too, but lacks stimulus. I find it elsewhere, looking, using my hour of freedom. I sit in Harry's Bar if it rains, walking through the square afterwards, under dripping trees, past the empty benches. Miriam Goldsmith, my eye sees fleetingly, my foot treading sodden leaves on wet gravel. Green streaks running down the white stone bearing up the statue still, with winter coming. I do want a child, soon.

I took a walk by the river today. It was too cold to sit out of doors, too windy, so I set off for the embankment. The water was rather choppy, this sudden, open expanse of dark grey under a grey sky, stretching freely. Buildings rising on the shoreline. Whenever I stand by the river or, better still, see the city from the water, I am conscious of the city as history. Seen from the water, this could be any city really, and landmarks are incidental. Stockholm or Petersburg in a northern light, according to the light. Fluid, buildings rising and falling, hence the sense of timelessness too, co-existing with history. Odd, this. When I stand looking at a historic monument I see just this, a heap of redundant rubbish, quaint, archaic, dead stone upon stone, inert. But a city held between water and sky, stretching into infinity, this says everything to me. Such insubstantiality, but so human. Held in the moment, all of us, between earth and water and sky.

Sweet Thames run softly till I end my song. This the continuum, our myth. Mere history says it was never sweet, not now, not then. Probably an open sewer since the very first settlement. But Canaletto saw his eternal city gleaming in this light. Do I see with his eyes? And even Wordsworth was spellbound, turning his back on the green hills. Is it his thrill going through me, his words echoing still in my senses? This is the continuum too, words learnt in the classroom, this inescapable rhythm shaping thought, my thought, yours. Time past and time present merging as I look, as I think of what I am seeing, learnt words shaping every thought. I remember what I have read about it, this historic pageant of watermen and barges, kings flaunting their moment of glory with fanfares and gilding, their victims going to a barbaric death and even greater glory, with hindsight. I remember this, it is in the books. I do not think of it, not consciously, but I see with their eyes, wavering images held in water, the memory of it, words colouring everything, this running story. Told not only by those in the moment, of it, but retold unendingly, then, now, this running theme with variations, our glorious, inglorious history river, echoing. Playing with it, imagining its untold aspects, the fear of it, the smell of rot in the shadow beneath the arch, to death by water. Green slime clinging to old bulwarks, but fiction living, amidst absent wharves and warehouses, restoring whatever is lost, or might have been, mudlarks scavenging on the shoreline under a sky shrill with seagulls, hungry too. Drownings, survivors. Lost or found. However fleeting and fortuitous, that which is written is held. Firm. For us.

Surprisingly bright day, cold, but light bouncing off buildings, windows. I opt for lunch in the square, wrapped up against the cold. A wary pigeon is stalking round the bench, on the lookout for scraps. Footpaths thick with fallen leaves, bronzed gold by a receding sun. Pedestrians hurry by. It is getting too cold for tourists and courtship, but the statue gleams in sudden beauty. Its dark metal folds contrast with the smooth-cut plinth on which he stands, feet apart, far-seeing, erect. The stone looks whiter than usual, kinder. Through the bare branches of trees I see a bright blue sky, baby blue, not a cloud wisp anywhere. Winter is coming, but this day is a gift, unexpected, dazzling. I sit in it, with the sky rising endlessly, the pattern changing. It is necessary to say this, to pin it down, how I sit in the square with a pattern of leafless branches overhead, through which I see clear blue sky, with winter coming. It is Thursday, but not a Thursday no different from any other, no. I am happy, I am still young. I try to jot down just what it is about this particular moment, how I sit with Miriam Goldsmith etched in the wood of the bench, with sparrows now hopping lightly around my feet, finding crumbs in the gravel. I do not know whether I will ever read this, but I feel compelled to try, as best I can, to hold it, this moment, and this.

Part Five

I

Simon.

Simple Simon met a pieman. No.

Jonathan.

Makes me think of David and. I don't know why. David doesn't have the same effect.

David.

I'm not keen on David. Too soft.

Joshua.

It'll get shortened to Josh. Anyway, why are we going through so many Jewish names?

We can hardly call him Norman.

I wasn't suggesting it. Stop joking.

I wasn't joking.

Of course you were. Nobody would choose Norman.

Lots of people are called Norman.

That's the trouble. The wrong sort of people. Not our friends.

Now you're being snobbish.

No, I'm not. Besides, your mother would have a fit. Not choosing a Jewish name is one thing. You don't have to go to the other extreme.

I was only joking.

I know.

Peter?

No. I once had a crush on a boy called Peter. Don't remind me.

Why? Did he drop you?

No, I dropped him. He was awful. I can't think what I ever saw in him. It was too embarrassing, trying to get rid of him.

So Peter's out.

Definitely.

I didn't know you were a *femme fatale*.

I'm not. Put it down to youth and inexperience. I still feel a bit guilty about it.

Darling!

I quite fancy Nicholas.

Who's he?

As a name, stupid.

Mm. Nicholas. My best friend at school was called Nicholas. I don't know why we lost touch. I'm not sure it goes with Wolfson. And it'll get shortened to Nick.

Not necessarily.

Inevitably. And it sounds so affected if you make a point of not shortening a name. My son Anthony – please don't call him Tony. You can't protect him from the rough and tumble of everyday life.

No.

Perhaps we should go for one syllable.

John.

Paul.

Mark.

Too Anglo-Saxon.

Too boring. A name should have a bit of panache. A bit of individuality. Justin.

Prissy.

Why?

I don't know. It just sounds a bit namby-pamby to me.

I think it sounds rather dignified, sort of noble.

It reminds you of justice, that's why.

Maybe.

Probably comes from Justinian.

Who was he?

Can't remember. You're supposed to be the literary one. Anyway, does it matter?

I think it does. I mean, if a name has a meaning, I think we should know what it is. Imagine choosing a name, and then you find out it means 'the bald-headed one'.

I don't think it matters, not really. Any meaning is lost in the mists of time, usually.

Perhaps we should buy a book on it.

Okay.

I rather like Bruno. It has a touch of the Mediterranean about it. And you can't mess about with it.

I thought you were keen on meaning? It only means brown.

I talk to him constantly, my sweet William. It seems as natural as breathing. The words are a kind of lullaby, as I walk him up and down, as I see his eyelids rising and falling, rising and falling, soothing him. I lull him on a cloud of soft language, it wraps him round, comforting him. Through it he knows I am nearby, holding him, shielding him from the terror of unending chaos, a limitless vacuum of random sounds into which he was thrust so suddenly.

Each time his eyes open, I speak to him. I know he is listening intently. I know it by the slight frown puckering his brows, by the manner in which he tries to focus his new eyes to where the sound is coming from. His new blue eyes which have not yet found their colour, reflecting sky, not earth. My mouth has found its song, and I sing it unthinkingly, for him. I am not conscious of sounding foolish, even if, overheard, the words seem silly. It is for him I speak, in the language of the newly born. He must hear it now, his mother tongue.

To soothe him, I tell him wonderful things, moon and stars shining, three ships sailing across the sea. You shall have a fishy on a little dishy when the boat comes in. His room is papered in blue, with a pattern of snowy clouds. Look, I say, touching the bluebirds which hang from his ceiling, so the cardboard shapes dip and swing, almost flying. When I stand at the window with him I see moving clouds in his sky-coloured irises.

I never pick him up but I speak to him.

3

Promise me, Daniel had said during my pregnancy, that you won't talk to him the way my sister talks to Annabel.

Annabel has tootsie-wootsies. She sleeps in a room full of bunnie-wunnies, with a white bow-wow in her cot.

It was easy enough to laugh, in the old days.

I cannot comprehend, Daniel commented, how a rational, intelligent woman can go soft in the head.

The child is rather sweet.

That is not at issue. But, like the rest of us, it has toes.

Such pretty toes – pink and soft, with tiny nails like mother-of-pearl.

Don't you start. If my sister would only listen to herself.

Look at the dicky bird.

A little itsy-bitsy, just for Mummy.

In your tummy.

Now, listening to myself, I sound similar. Not so utterly foolish, but I hear the pitch changing, rising, a singsong lilt. Whose tummy is this? Whose tummy is

Mummy tickling? Suspense, expectation, result. William holds his breath, shrieks excitedly, never tiring of it. I count his toes, each piggy in turn, go round the garden of his soft palm, help him in finding, naming his ears, mouth, nose. Such fun.

The fun of it is unending. Now he is pointing at that which is unnamed, further off, not part of himself.

Clock, I say. Hickory dickory dock.

The clock in the living room, and the clock in the book.

Out walking he points to trees, dogs, prams, ducks in the pond. This infinity of things, so far unnamed. I continue to tell him of ducks, and dogs, and trees.

Animals, which interest him most, this is where I find language breaking down, foolishly conscious of dichotomy. William, with the eyes of innocence, recognises their autonomy, in this is their fascination, why he will not take his eyes from them, moving through space, sky or water. Cow, I will try, but the word sounds arbitrary, without resonance. Moo, I say, entering his world, without disjunction between naming and function, where all creatures co-exist equally, free of linguistic dominion, control.

So far only ducks are unambiguously known by name, tamed by feeding. For all their quacking, ducks are just ducks, coming obediently when crumbs are thrown, gathering at our beck and call. But that which is swift, immense, oblivious of us, or scary, following its own singularity of path, not ours, in this he acknowledges uniqueness, a quite separate subjectivity. And I, trying to teach him, re-assess as I speak, as I have for so long spoken, glibly subordinating the world to my tongue, I, subject, predicating everything to my will. But now, looking with my child's eyes, I glimpse a world of lost wonders, the prelapsarian spectacle, not yet colonised by language. Baa, I say, pointing to the sheep, in field or on paper, coming to an understanding with him. William has no difficulty with this, only if I try to insist on sheep. It is I who feels stupidly sheepish. Naming, I think, stops us thinking about things, by controlling, categorising. So Adam, having given names to every wild animal in the garden, got thrown out. Grrr, I say, pointing to the lion. William concurs. Grrr, he says, understanding his wild spirit, joyful. All things bright and beautiful, growling, purring, fluttering, flying. William looks with wide open eyes.

4

Bird, I say. Can you see the pretty bird?

I am standing at the window with him, holding him, his feet on the sill. His look follows the fluttering wings, the sudden feathery motion from roof gutter to branch.

The bird has flown into the tree, I say, touching the pane with the tip of my finger, there, where the tree is not, where my skin meets the resisting glass through which it beckons.

153

Isn't it a pretty tree? I say. It is fully in leaf now. I hear the tree singing.

The bird is singing in the tree, I tell him. Can you hear it?

His grey eyes have not yet found their colour. He puts his two palms flat on the window, his mouth to it, licking. The glass mists over, he looks studiously at the wetness he has put there with his tongue. I wipe it off.

Look at the tree, I say, how green it is. It is summer now.

It sings in the wind, sways, thick with leaf, with colour, gathering all light and colour into its growth.

Unsmiling, solemn, I see him staring out with gravity, watching, waiting. Now he is gazing at the tree, waiting for it to do something. It is making a rustling sound, chirping. No bird. He bangs the window: still no bird. Now his attention is caught by clouds drifting across the clear blue sky.

Sky, I say. See the pretty white clouds?

Watching him look, I see sky and cloud reflected in his eyes, fresh as rainwater caught in a stony hollow.

The clouds fly in the sky, I say. Bringing rain. But not today. Today is a beautiful day.

Morning light, everything cool, clearcut and cleanly fresh for now. Deep shadow under the tree, first light held in its spreading branches, glowing. I open a window and the fresh breath of it, this glorious morning, blows in. Now I hear birdsong.

Hear the pretty birds singing?

But William is watching a ladybird crawling up the pane. Intently, bemused. After staring for a moment he tries to touch it, pick it up. The ladybird unexpectedly begins to fly, producing wings as if by magic.

Let it go, I say. Nice ladybird. Mustn't hurt it.

Gone, says William.

Yes, I say, laughing. It's gone. That surprised you, didn't it?

Ladybird, ladybird, I sing. Fly away home.

William begins stamping his feet on the sill, dancing to what for him is music, then kicks the glass.

No, I say sharply.

A sparrow is hopping along the flat roof just below us.

Look, I whisper, pointing, touching the glass.

I hear him breathing, staring steadily, feel his weight increasing as I stand, holding him.

Hush, I whisper. I expect it's hungry.

But now a distracting sound nearby, a fly buzzing furiously.

Shoo, I say, waving my free hand. Horrid thing.

His weight is getting too much, so I put him down on the floor. William protests noisily.

No, I say. Things to do. How about breakfast?

Up, says William, raising both arms.

No, I say. Not now. Time for breakfast.

William flings himself on the floor.

5

William is screaming. He is lying on the floor, shrieking. Each time I come near him he begins to kick, drumming his heels on the floor. I am at the end of my tether, with no notion of how to bring this to a conclusion. I suspect that he, too, no longer knows why it started, or how to end it. Our dialogue has broken down, or rather, William is fed up with it, with forever hearing no, no with no reason, this reason being incomprehensible to him. Not understanding, lacking the necessary skill to negotiate, he gives up on speech and turns to body language, going rigid in my hands, flinging himself to the floor, rolling and turning from me. I try speaking to him, by turns sternly, soothingly, but now he is unwilling to listen, drowning the sound of me by screaming at a higher pitch. Impotent fury feeding on its own momentum. I stop trying. Even if I knew what wish I had failed to interpret correctly, what inchoate impulse I had left unfulfilled, I could not help him. He must be left until, worn out, he is ready to try speech.

6

No.

William is pulling books off the bottom shelf.

No.

I put down the iron as he succeeds in tugging Mansfield, then Melville to the floor. I make a dive for *Moby Dick*, its up-ended spine cracking, crushing its contents.

Not for you, I say, lovingly smoothing two pages, then shutting it. I still think Mansfield and Melville make odd bedfellows, but Daniel is a stickler for arranging books in alphabetical order. I prefer them according to style, period. That is how I did it before we lived together.

This is for you.

I give him *Dennis the Dolphin*, which has big pictures and very few words. William knows the story, and can turn the pages by himself. He also knows what a dolphin is, although he has not seen one in the flesh. Only on the page, or performing tricks on television. Surprising, till I remember I have not seen a whale either.

William holds up the book. He wants me to read the story to him.

No, I say. Mummy is busy. I thump the iron on Daniel's shirt.

William points to the dolphin, wagging his head earnestly. Ga, he says, a syllable which stands in for anything not yet known by name.

Dolphin, I say.

I think of dolphins swimming in clear water, racing the prow of a ship. I wish I could tell him of it. William is kissing Dennis's fat blue shape. This dolphin smiles convincingly, and lets a small boy ride him through the waves. Nice dolphin, friendly Dennis. The small boy is rescued on the last page.

I think: soon he will know of dinosaurs, no doubt talk constantly of them, without ever seeing a dinosaur treading the earth. But then I think: our ancestors saw no dragons. Did Melville see a white whale?

I fold Daniel's fifth shirt, tip up the iron. William is pulling papers from the lower shelf of the coffee table. An untidy profusion of magazines, newspapers, brochures, catalogues, professional journals. Also several outstanding invoices, half buried under the accumulation.

No, I shout, wishing I or Daniel had got round to sorting the stuff out. Hurriedly I push things back. William scrunches an old newspaper, begins to shred it. As it is several days old, I let him continue, then gather up the torn newsprint.

I unplug the iron, put it away in the utility room. When I return William is pulling the flex from the table lamp.

No, I shriek, picking him up, heart thudding with alarm. William begins to protest, kicking in mid-air, yelling mildly.

I pick up *Dennis the Dolphin*, hand it to him. But William flings it from him, shaking his head wildly. He is trying to free himself from my grasp, pulling, stretching. I pick up another book, open it.

A is for apple, I say, juicy and ripe.

William sits still, attentive, looking.

I glance at my watch. There are twenty-six letters in the alphabet, and only thirty minutes in the next half hour, by which time lunch should be in the oven.

Apple, says William pointing.

I hurriedly work my way through ball and cake, dog and elephant, who holds a bright red ball in his trunk.

Apple, says William.

No, ball.

G is for girl, holding a bright red hat.

Apple, says William firmly.

Hat, I say, tapping the top of his head.

I turn the page.

H is for hat that I wear on my head. Luckily this hat is not round. It has a brim, with a white ribbon. Even better, two eyes look out from under the brim. William gazes up at me.

No, I say, laughing. I'm not wearing a hat.

William rubs the top of his head.

Nor are you, I add.

I get up, put the book in his lap.

You read it, I say, knowing he can turn the pages. I switch on the oven, season the dead chicken.

K is for kangaroo, jumping about, I say loudly. Can you find him?

I look up, but William is not where I left him. He is pushing buttons on the video recorder.

No, I say.

Hurriedly I pick him up, offer him the brightly coloured plastic shapes which fit into each other. I attach a round piece to a straight one, leave him to it. Look at the kitchen clock as I put the bird in the oven. William has got up, is toddling towards me.

Hello, I say, rooting about in the vegetable tray. When I look up he is touching the oven door.

No! I yell, going for him. He begins to scream.

Hot, I say, as he kicks, arches his back. Do you want to burn yourself?

7

Now I see the world afresh. Naming it will not do. Chair, I call it, noticing how its stability depends on being sat upon, heavily. Not on his pulling, reaching, tipping. Doors swing blindly, bumping. Not a door if it is ajar, hinges ready to trap exploring fingers. Lethal wires and sockets are everywhere, must be guarded, shut off, a deadly invisibility ready to spring. No, I say, but let him play with the floor switch of the standing lamp. On, off, on, off. Finding out. But the standing lamp totters, so I pull him away. Not a toy, I say, shutting the kitchen drawers, full of sharp things. He opens them again, trying to put his foot in. If I turn away the drawers become steps for him. As for the staircase, it is a precipice, looking down, but he is ready enough to climb up it on all fours.

With him I rediscover the tough clarity of glass, the fluidity of water, sunlight moving up a wall. I feel, with him, the wind touching his face, and rediscover the principle of Archimedes in his bath. I see all things newly, with his eyes, how alien the butterfly, far clouds moving, light, dark. Naming things round the garden, I find such multiplicity, a welter of words, colours.

8

William is sitting on the floor, spinning the globe. In his other hand he holds the pencil sharpener, fashioned as a miniature globe.

Big, small, he says, spinning the globe, lifting the sharpener.

Big, small, he keeps repeating.

I watch him from the doorway, unseen.

9

Why is the sky blue?
Why is it not?
How many numbers are there?
Why can't I?
What happens when we die?
How old is Granny?
How old is that, really?
When can I have a bicycle?
How long is that, really?
What is an idea?
Why don't you just tell me?
What do you mean, you don't know?
Where were you born?

Where was Daddy born?
When can I go to America?
How do birds fly?
Why do I have to go to bed?
Is there really a God?
What makes it rain?
When will it snow?
How big is space?
Is he the real Father Christmas?
How does he know everybody's address?
Will it hurt?
Will you stay with me?
What happens when space stops?
What do you mean, it doesn't?
How do things float?
Why is it sinking?
What are you thinking about?
Why hasn't he got a home?
Why doesn't he get a job then?
Can Jamie stay the night?
How soon will I be grown up?
What is your favourite colour?
What is your favourite food?
What is a mortgage?
Can I have a bicycle soon?
What happened then?
If I have a dream, and you are in it, do you dream it
too?
Will you stay with me?
When can I get up?
Why won't it go away?
Will I die?

When will you die?

If you do die, can I have your radio?

Will you read me a story?

What happened then?

Do witches fly about every night?

Is it time to get up?

Why is it so dark?

Do you think there is a God?

Why can't I?

Why won't you let me?

Did you know that Gemma's father works in a bank?

Do you know the joke about the rabbit who got on a bus?

How does it work?

Why don't you listen to me?

Do you want to hear a secret?

Will you promise not to tell him?

What are stars made of?

Is the moon a star too?

Could I go there?

Shall I tell you what I think?

Why is it silly?

How do you know?

Who was the first person ever to know that?

Was that before I was born?

Can you buy me a book about it?

When?

Why not now?

Even if I ask you very, very nicely?

Even if I promise not to make a fuss at bedtime?

Suppose I do make a fuss?

If the world goes round and round why don't we fall off?

Why don't aeroplanes fall down then?

How does it work?

What did you say to Granny?

Do dogs think like us?

Can I go by myself?

Who was the first person ever born?

When can we go to the zoo?

Which shoes shall I wear?

Why won't you talk to me?

Why can't I?

Why not?

Why is it dangerous?

If you do it, why can't I?

When can I?

Can I have an ice cream?

Is it time?

When will it be time?

How much longer do I have to wait?

Where does electricity come from?

Why must I go to school?

What is the government?

Do they tell everybody what to do?

If you don't, what happens to you?

Will you read me a story?

If it is scary, will you leave the light on?

Where does it say that?

How did he know?

Do you think it is going to be all right in the end?

Is there really a tooth fairy?

How do you know it is going to rain tomorrow?

Can I make a wish?
How much does it cost? Is that a lot?
Who is the most important person in the world?
Why?
Are you important?
Why not?
Is Daddy important?
Can I be a doctor when I grow up?
How many years?
How old would I be then?
Will you still be alive?
Is Daddy rich?
Who is rich?
Why?
How does it work?
Why don't you know?
Could you buy me a book about it?

10

Once upon a time. In the middle of a dark wood. Three ghostly figures stood. Snow fell for seven days and seven nights, burying every path. It was so still he could hear his own breath turning to icicles. In the middle of the wood he found a house, but it seemed to be empty. Nobody answered his knocking, or came to the door. The windows were shuttered. In a clearing he found bread, a cloth spread for it, and a knife to cut it with, but no message. When night fell he tried to sleep, but heard eerie sounds coming from afar. A wolf howling through the trees, the warning hoot of an owl nearby. Strange dreams came to him in the night. But when he woke up at daybreak he could not remember the message. For days and nights he continued his journey, marking his footsteps with dry twigs. He met a beggar asking for alms, face hidden from him by a drooping hood. After he had given a small coin she unexpectedly spoke, telling him to follow the call of the wood pigeon. In a clearing, spread on a cloth of fine linen, he found a haunch of venison, but no message. Further on he found a sharp sword hanging from the branch of a tree, and took it. He heard the wood pigeon's call, echoing through the barren trees. Sometimes it seemed to him that the wood itself was crying out. Stooping to drink from a dark pool, he saw his own reflection looking back at him, the mouth opening and shutting. He found he could not quench his thirst. Day and night he sat by the pool, watching the light dying, seeing moon and stars held in its dark water. Silent fish swam in its depths, moving eerily. A fin, an eddy perhaps, but then profound stillness. He might have sat thus forever, hearing only the mournful cry of the wood pigeon, but a monstrous bear came near, roaring with fury. He cut off its head with his sword, whereupon the severed head spoke, reciting a riddle which must be answered. He picked up his sword and went on his way, following the marks which the bear had left in the snow. They led up a steep hill, where the trees grew sparse. Here he found a cloth of gold and silver spread upon the ground, and on it a crystal bowl filled with sparkling fruit. It was incredible, being cunningly shaped from emeralds and rubies, amethysts and yellow diamonds. The bear's unanswered riddle echoed in his head. He had spoken of food which cannot be consumed, passing from mouth to mouth. He listened for the cry of the wood pigeon but heard nothing, only the wind sighing in the treetops. By the edge of the wood he saw that night was falling, with stars beyond number visible in the sky. Where to go now? Featureless land stretched in every direction. Helpless, he stood on the rocky hilltop, looking up at the starry sky. That which speaks but utters no sound, the bear had said. And saw a star dropping to earth. And so he continued on his way, day and night, a black crow circling round his head. Thinking of the third part of the bear's riddle: that which builds high but uses no stone. Caw caw shrieked the crow, his only companion. When he saw a castle shimmering on the horizon he started to hurry. And is still hurrying.

II

I turn a page, then shut the book. Daniel has already switched off his light. I walk to the window and draw back the curtains, lifting the sash to let in the night air. At first I see only how the trees stand, looming, a dark mass at the far end of the garden, the yellow square of a lit window beyond. But slowly the dim night sky reveals itself, rising high over my head. A faint dusting of stars and the arc of a new moon throwing out a foggy halo, sky the colour of night.

I get back into bed.

There's a new moon, I say.

No reply.

The room is now flooded with ghostly light.

The new moon with the old moon in her arms, I murmur. Who said that?

No answer.

Are you asleep?

I hear him breathing, a sudden rush of wind in the trees.

I try to think of an adjective for the colour of night.

Vacant interstellar spaces, I think. O dark dark dark.

I am wide awake, looking out at the night. Beneath the visiting moon.

Silver fruit upon silver trees.

Who said that?

My head an echo chamber.

The silver apples of the moon.

Ink, I think, for the colour of night.

I cannot switch off. Try counting stars. Castor, Pollux. What was their story?

Every star with its story. Flung up into the night sky.

Andromeda, daughter of Cassiopeia.

Legends echoing, light years ago.

Are you there, star? Or is it only your light?

This mirror of death, speaking to us.

Out of the emptiness.

From out the vacant interstellar spaces.

Is there anybody out there? Send radio signals into the void.

Bleep bleep.

I do wish Daniel would wake up. I want to talk.

Count a few more stars. Betelgeuse.

Man hath weav'd out a net, and this net thrown upon the heavens, and now they are his own.

If only Daniel would speak to me. I hear him turning, muttering under his breath.

Poor old moon, are you lonely up there, circling in the void? Ancient, pock-marked. No sign of Endymion.

Venus. The Great Bear.

Bleep bleep. Think of it, the possibility of a faint signal out of the dark.

Naming it, the void. Trying to find our way in the dark, so as not to be utterly lost.

The cry of a night owl, hollow, woodwind calling.

Naming it, longing and terror.

If he will not wake, I must go on speaking to myself. My head clear as the night sky, seeing moonlight in my bedroom mirror. Words crowding in.

Bleep bleep. What would they tell us, from the far edge of things?

Perseus. The North Star.

Finding our way in the dark. Through that which was without form, and void.

Wake up, speak to me.

I hear his breathing, heavy and slow.

Orion, his belt, his sword.

A giant step, but not for mankind.
No.
Cry of the night owl, mournful.
O dark dark dark.
Speak to me, please.